COLLINS

AIRCRAFT
OF
WW II

Jane's

month later Navy
in New Geor...
Modi...

d operations

USA

'ralia
ince
nce
nd
aly
ty
y

55

...century. An ...precedented number of aircraft were built at staggering expense. The United States, United Kingdom, Soviet Union, Germany, Japan and Italy built over 750,000 aircraft between 1939 ...

INVESTIGATING
CLIMATE
CHANGE

INVESTIGATING CLIMATE CHANGE

SCIENTISTS' SEARCH FOR ANSWERS IN A WARMING WORLD

REBECCA L. JOHNSON

Caption for image on page 2: Scientists created this false-color image of Earth using data gathered by the CERES instruments on NASA's Terra spacecraft. (CERES stands for Clouds and the Earth's Radiant Energy System.) The image shows where more heat (red to orange) or less heat (blue to white) is radiating from Earth's atmosphere. The blue patches are the frigid tops of high clouds.

Twenty-First Century Books
A division of Lerner Publishing Group, Inc.
241 First Avenue North
Minneapolis, MN 55401 U.S.A.

Website address: www.lernerbooks.com

Library of Congress Cataloging-in-Publication Data

Johnson, Rebecca L.
  Investigating climate change: scientists' search for answers in a warming world / by
Rebecca L. Johnson.
    p.   cm. — (Discovery!)
  Includes bibliographical references and index.
  ISBN 978–0–8225–6792–9 (lib. bdg. : alk. paper)
    1. Climatic changes—Juvenile literature. 2. Climatic changes—Environmental aspects—
Juvenile literature. I. Title.
  QC981.8.C5J64 2009
  551.6—dc22   2007038566

Manufactured in the United States of America
1 2 3 4 5 6 – DP – 14 13 12 11 10 09

CONTENTS

INTRODUCTION / 7

CHAPTER ONE
GLACIERS, THE GREENHOUSE EFFECT,
AND CARBON DIOXIDE / 11

CHAPTER TWO
ANCIENT CLUES AND CLIMATE MODELS / 25

CHAPTER THREE
MELTING ICE AND RISING SEAS / 45

CHAPTER FOUR
ALTERED ECOSYSTEMS, ENDANGERED SPECIES,
AND EXTREME WEATHER / 65

CHAPTER FIVE
THE CHALLENGE OF A WARMER WORLD / 85

GLOSSARY / 100

SOURCE NOTES / 104

SELECTED BIBLIOGRAPHY / 10

FURTHE

INTRODUCTION

Bruce Molnia peered through his camera lens. Then he glanced at the black-and-white photo in his hand. The old photo showed Muir Glacier in Alaska's Glacier Bay National Park. William Field had taken it on this very spot in 1941. Sixty-three years later, Molnia was photographing the same scene. The two photos would be very different. In 1941 the icy edge of Muir Glacier had been a few feet from the camera. In 2004 it wasn't even visible from this spot. It had retreated beyond the camera's view. The only glacier Molnia could see was Riggs Glacier, far off in the distance.

Between 1941 and 2004, a large part of Muir Glacier melted. The front of the glacier retreated more than 7 miles (11 kilometers). The glacier also thinned by more than 2,625 feet (800 meters). Where a thick river of ice had once crept between mountain peaks, a deep ocean inlet remained. Trees and shrubs grew above the waterline.

Molnia is a glacial geologist with the U.S. Geological Survey. He tracks down old photos of Alaskan glaciers. He travels to those glaciers and photographs them again. He and other scientists compare

The changes are shocking. In less than one hundred years, at least 95 percent of the glaciers in Alaska have retreated. They've melted especially fast since about 1990.

Alaska isn't the only place where a lot of ice is melting quickly. Mountain glaciers on other continents are retreating too. In Greenland and Antarctica, vast ice sheets are shrinking and thinning. In the Arctic, sea ice is disappearing.

Scientists worldwide agree that the main cause of all this melting is global warming. Global warming is a rise in Earth's average surface temperature. Since 1900 Earth's average surface temperature has warmed 1.4°F (0.8°C). Most of that warming has happened since the early 1980s. Eleven of the twelve years from 1995 to 2007 were the hottest years on record.

Over millions of years, Earth's average surface temperature has warmed and cooled many times. Such changes are part of the planet's natural cycles. But global warming is different. It's happening very quickly. It's not part of a natural cycle. Global warming is happening largely because of human activities. These activities are intensifying (strengthening) Earth's natural warming processes.

Scientists and many other people are very concerned about global warming. That's because global warming can change Earth's climate. Climate is a region's average weather over a very long time. Climate depends on things that happen simultaneously in the air, in the oceans, and on land. Climate tends to stay the same for hundreds, thousands, or even tens of thousands of years. It can and does change. But typically, climate change is very slow and gradual.

Earth's current situation isn't typical. Scientists have gathered strong evidence that global warming is already changing Earth's climate. And this climate change is occurring fast. Some changes, such as melting glaciers, are visible within a human

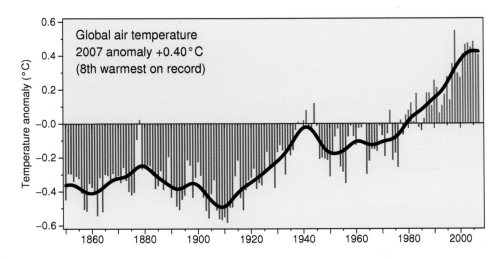

This graph shows the upward trend in Earth's average surface tem-
perature. Global warming began intensifying in the early 1980s. An
anomaly is a deviation from what is normal or expected.

lifetime. "What we're seeing," says Molnia, "is the response of
one part of the Earth's surface environment—the glaciers—to
changes in climate." Climate change affects more than just ice,
water, land, and air. It affects plants, animals, and people too. It
can affect every being on Earth.

Concerns about global warming and climate change might
seem new. But thoughtful researchers were ~~thinking~~
about ~~global~~

CHAPTER ONE

GLACIERS, THE GREENHOUSE EFFECT, AND CARBON DIOXIDE

To a patient scientist, the unfolding greenhouse mystery is far more exciting than the plot of the best mystery novel. But it is slow reading, with new clues sometimes not appearing for several years. Impatience increases when one realizes that it is not the fate of some fictional character, but of our planet and species, which hangs in the balance as the great carbon mystery unfolds at a seemingly glacial pace.

—David W. Schindler, "The Mysterious Missing Sink"

Glaciers sparked the first scientific interest in climate change. In the early 1800s, scientists concluded that many mount glaciers were remnants of the "ice age." They age was a cold period in Earth's riod, enormous glaci equator. I

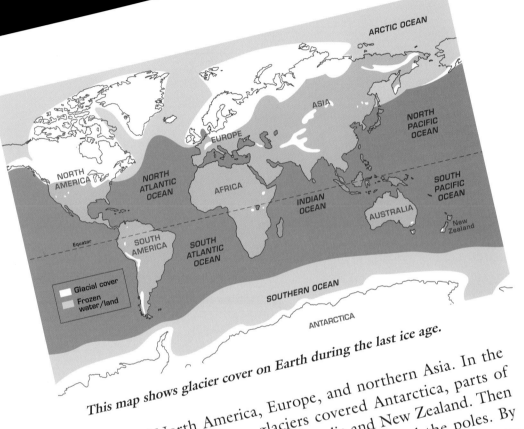

This map shows glacier cover on Earth during the last ice age.

much of North America, Europe, and northern Asia. In the Southern Hemisphere, glaciers covered Antarctica, parts of South America, and parts of Australia and New Zealand. Then slowly, the vast glaciers retreated back toward the poles. By about ten thousand years ago, the only ice left was on mountaintops and near the poles.

How did nineteenth-century scientists reach this conclusion? They studied evidence the glaciers left behind. Deep scratches in solid bedrock showed how glaciers had moved. Certain kinds of hills and valleys showed where glaciers had pushed up or gouged out the land. Many of the gouges had filled with water to become lakes.

Before this study of glaciers, most people believed that Earth's climate had always been about the same. Evidence of advancing and retreating glaciers showed that Earth's climate could change. Earth had once been cold enough for glaciation (formation of continent-size glaciers) to occur. Later, the planet had warmed enough to melt most of that ice.

Eventually scientists realized that glaciation had happened many times. That meant that Earth's climate had changed many times too. Repeatedly, the planet's average surface temperature had risen and fallen over long periods of time. But scientists couldn't explain how this had happened. They puzzled over what could possibly change Earth's climate so drastically.

Many nineteenth-century scientists tried to solve the mystery of glaciation. They proposed a variety of explanations for climate change. Some suggested that the sun is hotter at times. Others thought that Earth periodically moves closer to or farther from the sun. Still others proposed that Earth itself goes through some kind of natural temperature cycle. Scientists hotly debated these hypotheses.

THE ATMOSPHERE AND THE GREENHOUSE EFFECT

In the 1820s, French scientist Jean-Baptiste Joseph Fourier proposed a different idea. He thought that a change in Earth's atmosphere (blanket of gases) could trigger climate change.

Fourier was convinced that the atmosphere controls glob
surface temperature. Sunlight continually heats E
Yet Earth doesn't just get hotter an
that Earth must lose som
keeps enough

OUR GLOBAL GREENHOUSE

The sun constantly radiates (sends out) enormous amounts of energy. Part of solar energy is visible light. Visible light is energy we can see. We cannot see other parts of solar energy. For example, infrared radiation (heat) and ultraviolet radiation (which causes sunburn) are forms of solar energy that are invisible to humans.

Solar energy passes easily through Earth's atmosphere. Snow, ice, and clouds reflect some of this energy directly back to space. But land, water, trees, buildings, and other objects absorb a great deal of solar energy.

As Earth's surface absorbs energy, the surface warms up. The warm surface radiates heat. Some of this heat escapes directly to space. But certain atmospheric gases (greenhouse gases) absorb some of the heat. These gases reradiate the heat they absorb. They do this again and again. The overall effect is to trap heat in the atmosphere.

This heat-trapping process is the greenhouse effect. Scientists gave it this name because the heat-trapping ability of the atmosphere resembles the heat-trapping ability of a greenhouse. In a greenhouse, solar energy passes through the structure's clear covering. The solar energy warms the objects inside the greenhouse. The warm objects radiate heat. But that heat can't escape the greenhouse. So the temperature inside the greenhouse rises. Earth's greenhouse effect is a bit more complicated. But the end result is an Earth much warmer than it would be without its heat-trapping atmosphere. Scientists estimate that without its atmosphere, Earth's average surface temperature would be about –2.2°F (–19°C). That's far too cold to support life on Earth as we know it.

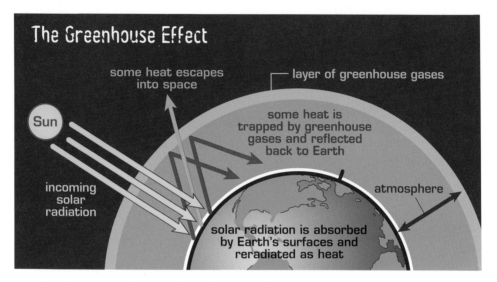

Earth's atmosphere (enlarged in this diagram) acts somewhat like the clear covering of a greenhouse. It lets solar energy reach Earth's surface and then traps some of the reradiated heat.

CARBON DIOXIDE

Around 1859 Irish scientist John Tyndall identified two greenhouse gases that are especially good at trapping heat. One is water vapor—the invisible, gaseous form of water. The other greenhouse gas Tyndall identified is carbon dioxide.

Nineteenth-century scientists were familiar with ~~~~ dioxide. They knew that this colorl~~~ portant part of life ~~ living ~~~

Living plants, algae, and some types of one-celled organisms (living things) take in carbon dioxide. They absorb it from air or water. They use the gas in photosynthesis. In this process, organisms change carbon dioxide and water into sugar and oxygen.

Scientists call carbon dioxide by its chemical name, CO_2. A molecule of CO_2 (the smallest possible particle of CO_2) is made of three atoms (units of matter): two oxygen atoms (O_2) and one carbon atom (C).

Carbon is a very common substance on Earth. The oceans contain vast amounts of carbon. Some of it is dissolved in the water. Large amounts are in thick sediment (mud) on the ocean floor. All living things contain carbon. And since dead organisms often become part of soil, soil contains a lot of carbon too.

THE CARBON CYCLE

Carbon doesn't stay put. Over time, it cycles (travels) through the natural world. Carbon moves from place to place on Earth through the carbon cycle. Some carbon moves through the cycle fairly quickly. For example, as trees in a forest carry out photosynthesis, they take in CO_2. Thus, carbon that was in the air goes into molecules that form the trees' trunks, branches, leaves, and roots. If the forest catches fire or if a storm blows down the trees so they die and decay, the trees will release CO_2. Much of the carbon the trees contained will go back into the air.

Some carbon moves through the cycle very slowly. Rich deposits of carbon lie deep underground. These deposits formed from animals and plants that died millions of years ago. Water or sediment covered these dead organisms before they decayed.

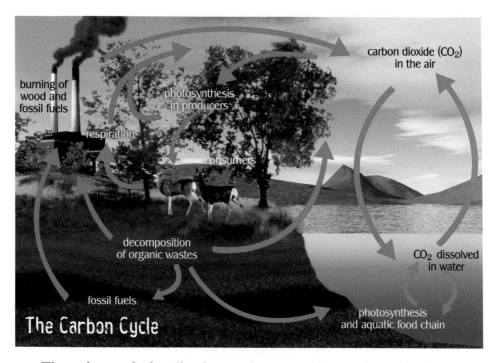

burning of
wood and
fossil fuels

photosynthesis
in producers

respiration

consumers

carbon dioxide (CO_2)
in the air

decomposition
of organic wastes

CO_2 dissolved
in water

fossil fuels

photosynthesis
and aquatic food chain

The Carbon Cycle

The carbon cycle describes how carbon moves into and out of different parts of the global environment.

The buried remains gradually turned into fossil fuels (coal, oil, and natural gas). Fossil fuels contain huge amounts of carbon. When they burn, most of the carbon they contain moves into the air in CO_2 molecules.

Hogbom tried to calculate approximately how much carbon moved from one part of the carbon cycle to another. To do this, he had to estimate how much CO_2 moves into and out of the atmosphere from all processes. Hogbom knew that natural processes put some CO_2 in the air. For example, forest fires and volcanic eruptions release CO_2. He also recognized an unnatural source of atmospheric CO_2: coal-powered factories. In Hogbom's day, factories were burning tens of millions of tons of coal each year.

Most people saw the black smoke coming from factory smokestacks as a sign of progress. Hogbom realized the factories were releasing CO_2 into the atmosphere. He didn't know exactly how much. But he estimated that burning fossil fuels was adding about as much CO_2 to the air as all natural processes combined.

Smoke billows into the air at this coal-burning power station in Yunnan, China, in 2007. Coal-burning power stations release vast amounts of CO_2 into the atmosphere.

Hogbom's colleague, Swedish chemist Svante August Arrhenius, was interested in atmospheric CO_2 for different reasons. Arrhenius was trying to solve the continuing mystery of ice ages and climate change.

In the mid-1890s, Arrhenius proposed that a change in the atmosphere could alter Earth's climate enough to cause an ice age. If the atmospheric CO_2 concentration decreased, the greenhouse effect would weaken. Earth's average surface temperature would fall. If the temperature dropped low enough, this global cooling would trigger glaciation.

Arrhenius also suggested that increased atmospheric CO_2 could intensify the greenhouse effect. Earth's average surface temperature would rise. This global warming would lead to a variety of climate changes.

Around that time, American geologist T. C. Chamberlain independently reached the same conclusion as Arrhenius had. Neither scientist was worried about it. Both assumed global warming wouldn't happen for many centuries.

Why so long? Scientists knew that oceans absorb a lot of CO_2 from the atmosphere. Photosynthesizing organisms absorb some too. Arrhenius and Chamberlain believed that natural processes would remove most of the "extra" CO_2 that burning fossil fuels added to the air.

Other scientists agreed. Rising CO_2
an immediate problem

temperature records dating back to 1900. The records revealed a clear warming trend. Callendar then tracked down the best available measurements of atmospheric CO_2 for the same period. He discovered that CO_2 had increased by about 10 percent. He concluded that burning fossil fuels had added enough atmospheric CO_2 to raise Earth's average surface temperature.

Callendar published a paper titled "The Artificial Production of Carbon Dioxide and Its Influence on Temperature." In the paper, he firmly linked increasing atmospheric CO_2 with global warming. But few scientists accepted this idea. They doubted the old measurements Callendar had found were accurate. And most of them still believed the oceans would absorb excess CO_2 from the atmosphere.

TRACKING FOSSIL CARBON

Then, in the 1950s, scientists developed carbon-14 dating. Using this method, scientists can determine something's age by measuring its carbon-14 content. Carbon-14 is a kind of carbon atom. Most of Earth's carbon atoms are carbon-12. Carbon-14 atoms are rare, but they constantly form in the upper atmosphere. They make their way down to Earth's surface, where they enter the carbon cycle.

Carbon-14 atoms are radioactive. They release energy as they gradually break down. Carbon-14 breaks down at a constant, known rate. So something that contains a lot of carbon-14 is relatively young. Something that contains little or no carbon-14 is much older. Fossil fuels contain no carbon-14. All the carbon-14 they once contained broke down long ago.

American chemist Hans Suess realized that carbon-14 dating could help scientists follow carbon as it moved through the carbon cycle. Using that method, in 1955 Suess discovered something surprising in wood from living trees. Trees take up CO_2 from the air during photosynthesis. The carbon from CO_2 molecules ends up in tree tissues, including wood. Suess found that his wood samples contained far less carbon-14 than he had expected. He deduced that all the atmospheric carbon-12 from fossil fuels was diluting the atmospheric concentration of carbon-14.

Suess was excited by this discovery. He had tracked "fossil carbon" moving from the atmosphere into plants. Could he track fossil carbon moving from the atmosphere into the ocean? If so, scientists could better estimate how much atmospheric CO_2 the oceans were absorbing.

Roger Revelle, an expert on ocean chemistry, joined Suess in studying carbon atoms in the oceans. Revelle was the director of the Scripps Institution of Oceanography in California.

Revelle and Suess took many seawater samples and ran many tests. The results were clear—and unexpected. The ocean did absorb atmospheric CO_2, as scientists had long believed. But the water's chemistry changed in the process. Seawater that contained some CO_2 resisted absorbing more. In fact, it soon began releasing CO_2 back into the air. It released almost as much as it absorbed. In other words, the ocean wasn't removing the huge amounts of CO_2 people were adding to the air by burning fossil f

The two

Revelle and Suess published an article about their ocean studies. In it they wrote that by adding huge amounts of CO_2 to the atmosphere, "human beings are now carrying out a large-scale geophysical experiment" on Earth.

This article convinced a few scientists that Callendar might have been right. Perhaps CO_2 was collecting in the atmosphere. But how much was up there? And how fast was its concentration increasing? To answer these questions, scientists needed reliable measurements of atmospheric CO_2.

KEELING AND GLOBAL CO$_2$

That task fell to a young American geochemist, Charles David Keeling. Keeling was working at the California Institute of Technology. As part of his research there, he had developed an accurate system for measuring CO_2 concentration in air. He used the system to analyze air samples from study sites in forests and other natural settings. In 1956 Revelle persuaded Keeling to come to Scripps and tackle the problem of measuring atmospheric CO_2.

The job was very challenging. Before, Keeling had measured CO_2 levels in small, relatively confined areas. Measuring atmospheric CO_2 levels required sampling Earth's air on a global scale. Those air samples had to be as clean as possible, so the CO_2 measurements would be accurate. That meant Keeling needed to collect air samples far from cities, highways, factories, and all other possible sources of air pollution.

Keeling began his research in 1958. He worked from ships at sea and monitoring stations in remote parts of the world. One of these stations was on top of Mauna Loa, a mountain on the island of Hawaii. Mauna Loa rises more than 2.5 miles (4 km) above the central Pacific Ocean.

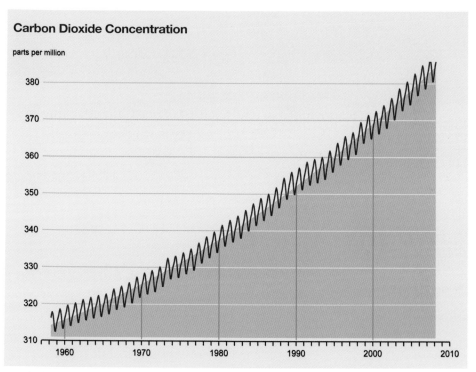

Carbon Dioxide Concentration

parts per million

This graph shows the steady increase in atmospheric CO$_2$ since monitoring began in the late 1950s. Scientists often call this graph the Keeling Curve.

Keeling was able to get very precise measurements of global atmospheric CO$_2$. After just two

CHAPTER TWO
ANCIENT CLUES
AND CLIMATE MODELS

The farther backward you can look, the farther forward you are likely to see.

—Winston Churchill, prime minister of England, 1940–1945 and 1951–1955

Throughout the 1970s, Keeling's research on atmospheric carbon dioxide continued. Without fail, the concentration of this gas in the atmosphere kept rising. More scientists began paying attention to this relentless increase in a greenhouse gas. They wondered how all that CO_2 might affect Earth. Was increasing CO_2 really intensifying the greenhouse effect, as Callendar had suggested? Was Earth's average surface temperature rising as CO_2 collected in the atmosphere? If so, by how much and how quickly? Was the warming due only to increasing atmospheric CO_2? Or were other factors at work too?

THE INSTRUMENT RECORD

Scientists tackled the tempera
average surface temp

more than a century's worth of temperature data. The data came from three different types of instruments.

The thermometer is the simplest and oldest instrument used to measure temperature. The first modern thermometers appeared in the 1700s. By the mid-1800s, scientists were using them regularly to record air temperature. So were many weather enthusiasts. Sailors used thermometers to measure air temperature at sea. They also measured the temperature of surface waters.

In the 1930s, the world gained another tool for measuring air temperature: the radiosonde. A radiosonde is a small package containing a thermometer and several other instruments. A balloon carries it up through the atmosphere. As it rises, its instruments measure temperature, humidity, and air pressure at different altitudes. The radiosonde sends this information via radio signals to receivers on the ground.

By the 1940s, scientists were launching radiosondes daily from hundreds of weather stations and ships around the world. They even launched radiosondes from very remote places such as Antarctica, where no one had been able to measure air temperature before. In 1957 and 1958, scientists set up many new weather stations as part of the International Geophysical Year.

A third temperature-gathering tool appeared in the 1970s. Satellites began measuring Earth's surface temperature from space. Satellites don't measure temperature directly. Rather, they measure the infrared radiation coming from the planet's surface. Researchers convert these energy measurements into temperatures.

The scientists studying Earth's temperature trends combined all the data from thermometers, radiosondes, and satellites.

They used these data to estimate global average surface temperature from the mid-1800s to the early 1980s.

Plotted on a graph, the data painted an interesting picture. Although there were fluctuations (slight ups and downs), Earth's average surface temperature had generally warmed from the middle of the 1800s until the 1940s. From the 1940s to the early 1970s, it had cooled slightly. After the mid-1970s, Earth had resumed its warming trend.

The mid-century temperature dip was puzzling. Keeling's data showed that atmospheric CO_2 had climbed steadily during that time. If atmospheric CO_2 affected global temperature, why hadn't temperature readings risen along with increasing CO_2? Despite this mystery, the general trend in global surface temperature was obvious. The instrument record showed a gradual but definite rise in Earth's average surface temperature since the mid-1800s.

THE MYSTERIOUS COOLING

Scientists eventually explained Earth's mysterious mid-1900s cooling. At that time, air pollution was a growing problem worldwide. Air pollution includes tiny particles called aerosols, which block sunligh[t]
ing roughly the same period, an unusually large num[ber]
erupted. Volcanic eruptions blast aerosols hig[h]
a few decades, all these aerosols e[
This shading effect counter[
stricter pollution [
sols. Ae[

CLUES FROM THE PAST

Both atmospheric CO_2 and global temperature had increased since the mid-1800s. A growing number of scientists suspected that CO_2 was linked to the warming. But they needed concrete proof. They eventually found it in Earth's distant past.

In the 1970s, scientists began building a detailed record of Earth's paleoclimate (ancient climate). The data for this record came from many different sources.

In areas with temperate climates (warm summers and cool winters), many trees add a layer of new wood to their trunks every summer. Climate affects this layer's thickness. Trees grow thicker layers during warmer, wetter summers. They grow thinner layers during cooler, drier summers.

When people cut a tree's trunk crosswise, the layers of wood appear as concentric rings (circles with a common center). The oldest rings are near the center. Moving out from the center,

The rings of a tree can show what the climate was like during each year of the tree's life.

the rings are increasingly recent. The outermost ring formed in the last year of the tree's life.

The size and condition of each tree ring provide clues about the climate during the year it formed. Some trees can live many centuries. Paleoclimatologists study rings in cross sections of very old trees (after the trees die) or extract and examine cores (thin cylinders of wood) from living trees. The rings tell what the climate was like in the trees' habitats during their lifetime.

Flowering plants produce dustlike grains called pollen. Pollen contains reproductive cells that help plants make seeds. Each kind of flowering plant has unique pollen. If you can identify the types of pollen found in a certain place, then you know what kinds of plants grow there. This, in turn, can tell a great deal about the climate. For example, pollen from cactus indicates a dry, hot climate—the conditions necessary for a cactus to grow.

Pollen can tell a lot about ancient climates too. Pollen is tough. It can survive for hundreds—even thousands—of years. Pollen falls to the ground and mixes with soil. It also washes or blows into lakes, where it settles to the lake bottom. Year after year, the tiny grains collect in layers of soil and lake sediments. They provide a record of the plants growing in a place over time.

Paleoclimatologists use pollen in soil and lake sediments as clues to Earth's past climate. These scientists extract sediments from many locations. They identify the pollen in the sedime Then they deduce what the climates of those l like long ago.

Paleoclimatologists worki rings, pollen, an to be

Some types of pollen can survive for hundreds of thousands of years. But like tree rings, pollen samples reflect the climate of only one area. Scientists building the paleoclimatic record needed older and more global clues about Earth's climate. To find these clues, scientists used methods based on a discovery from the 1950s.

In the 1950s, nuclear chemist Harold Urey from the University of Chicago was studying oxygen atoms. Urey discovered that the ratio of different kinds of oxygen atoms in air depends on air temperature. Like CO_2, atmospheric oxygen dissolves in ocean water. When ocean organisms take in oxygen, the different kinds of oxygen atoms become part of their bodies. When the organisms die, the parts of their bodies that don't decay, such as shells, preserve the oxygen atoms.

Foraminifera, commonly called forams, are tiny, shelled organisms that live by the trillions in oceans worldwide. When forams die, their shells settle to the ocean floor. They pile up in ocean sediments year after year.

Paleoclimatologists realized that foram shells in ocean sediments might reveal a lot about ancient global temperatures. So the scientists extracted sediment samples from all the world's oceans. They lowered special drills from ships to the seabed and cut out long cylinders, or cores, of ocean sediments.

The ocean floor sediments had collected in layers. The youngest layers were on top. The oldest layers were on the bottom. Paleoclimatologists used carbon-14 dating to learn the age of each layer. Very deep cores contained layers that were hundreds of thousands of years old. Scientists analyzed the ratio of different kinds of oxygen atoms in each layer's foram shells.

When scientists combined information from all the layers, they could see how Earth's average surface temperature had

A scientist studies a sediment core from the ocean at Woods Hole Oceanographic Institution in Massachusetts.

changed over time. They identified long cold periods, when glaciers must have covered much of the planet. Cold periods gave way to warm periods, when there was far less ice on Earth. Thanks to ancient forams, paleoclimatologists could draw a time line of Earth's glaciations and interglacial periods. This record of climate change dated back several hundred thousand years.

A picture of Earth's past climate changes was gradually emerging. But scientists were still searching for a link between climate and atmospheric CO_2. They found it in ice.

THE ICE CORE CONNECTION

Ice cores are long
Ice c

Greenland and Antarctica have the thickest, oldest ice. Working in temperatures often well below 0°F (−18°C), scientists began drilling extremely long cores from both places in the late 1970s and early 1980s. They also collected ice cores from mountain glaciers all over the world. In frigid labs, they dated the layers. The longest cores, from the polar regions, dated back hundreds of thousands of years.

Then scientists studied the air bubbles in the ice. The bubbles revealed the atmospheric CO_2 concentration when each layer formed. By measuring the ratio of different kinds of oxygen atoms in the trapped air, scientists also determined a rough measure of the air temperature when each layer formed. In short, ice cores held linked clues to both air temperature and atmospheric CO_2 over time. Climate scientists were especially excited to discover that Northern Hemisphere ice core data matched Southern Hemisphere data. The match meant that the climate changes recorded in ice had occurred worldwide.

A glaciologist holds an ice core just drilled from the ice sheet at Law Dome camp in East Antarctica.

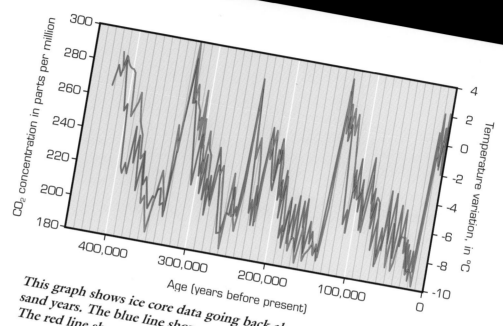

This graph shows ice core data going back about four hundred thousand years. The blue line shows global average surface temperature. The red line shows atmospheric CO_2 levels. The data is from an ice core drilled at the Russian research station Vostok in Antarctica.

As scientists analyzed ice core data, they discovered an important relationship. Atmospheric CO_2 and global surface temperature had risen and fallen together for hundreds of centuries. The scientists didn't know if increasing CO_2 caused the warming periods recorded in the ice. The data didn't reveal cause and effect. But the close link between CO_2 changes and temperature changes underscored CO_2's significance in the process of global warming.

NATURAL CLIMATE-CHANGING FORCES

As paleoclimatolo

Aerosols from a huge eruption can block enough solar energy to cool Earth slightly. This cooling can last for several years.

Global winds and ocean currents carry heat from the equator toward the poles. These circulation patterns influence climate worldwide. When the patterns change, so does climate. One such change is the El Niño Southern Oscillation (ENSO). ENSO is a set of wind and water changes in the Pacific Ocean.

In the tropical Pacific, winds typically push surface waters westward, toward Australia and Indonesia. This keeps the western Pacific warmer and the eastern Pacific cooler. Roughly every three to seven years, the winds weaken. This lets warmer western Pacific water head east, toward South America. This is the beginning of an El Niño event. Warmer, moister air moves east with the warmer water. Rains and floods increase in South America. Indonesia and Australia experience droughts.

La Niña, another event, often follows. During La Niña, westward-blowing winds strengthen. Warmer waters concentrate even more in the west, and cooler waters in the east. Indonesia and Australia have floods during La Niña. Western South America often has terrible droughts.

Changes in Earth's tilt on its axis affect climate, and so do changes in Earth's orbit around the sun. Earth's orbit varies from nearly circular to slightly elliptical (oval). This sequence of variations is called an orbital cycle. Earth completes one orbital cycle every one hundred thousand years or so. The annual average distance between Earth and the sun changes as Earth's orbit changes. When Earth is closer to the sun, the planet is slightly warmer. When Earth is farther away, it's cooler.

The sun changes too. The amount of energy it gives off varies. This is due mostly to sunspots, cooler patches that form on the sun's surface. When the sun has many sunspots, slightly less solar energy reaches Earth. Sunspots wax and wane over roughly an eleven-year cycle.

CLIMATE MODELS

While paleoclimatologists looked back in time to understand Earth's climate, other scientists during the 1970s and 1980s looked forward. They built models of Earth's climate system. They hoped these climate models would not only help them understand how climate works but also help them predict future climate change.

Climate models are very complex computer programs. Scientists create them using mathematical equations. They divide Earth's surface and atmosphere into cells (three-dimensional blocks). Then they develop sets of equations that describe the conditions in each cell. These equations reflect how temperature, humidity, wind speed, and many other factors play a role in climate. More equations link all the cells so they operate together, as Earth's climate system does.

The "ancestors" of climate models were early weather models. Scientists developed the first weather models 1950s, when digital

Then the computer ran the model again. This time it started with the solutions to the first set of calculations instead of current weather data. This process continued until the model predicted the weather for the next day or two. Computers in the 1950s were horribly slow. Early weather models took so long to run that they barely kept up with the real weather!

During the 1960s, both weather models and computers improved. Computers not only ran faster but were able to process more complex data. A better understanding of weather patterns and access to more kinds of weather data led to better, more complex weather models. These models helped scientists make fairly accurate short-range weather predictions.

Predicting long-range climate change, however, was far more challenging than predicting tomorrow's weather. Teams of researchers began developing climate models in the 1960s. But these models were very limited—both by the quality of climate data and by computer power.

It wasn't until the mid to late 1970s that the first reasonably accurate climate models came along. By that time, scientists had a better understanding of several key climate processes. They also had enough climate data to begin constructing models that represented real-world climate behavior fairly well. Much of that data came from new scientific instruments, such as satellite sensors. These new tools provided more and better information about the atmosphere, the ocean, and other parts of Earth's climate system.

Different teams of scientists developed slightly different climate models. But as a group, they were all general circulation models (GCMs). The word *circulation* refers to the basic ways in which air circulates throughout Earth's atmosphere. Mathematically, the models described how rain falls and evaporates from land.

They described how solar energy passes through the atmosphere. They also described how heat rising from Earth's surface interacts with certain greenhouse gases. However, the GCMs of the late 1970s and early 1980s did not describe how the atmosphere and oceans interact. And they didn't include the effects of clouds on climate. These flaws were unavoidable. Scientists simply had no reliable data about these processes at the time.

Nevertheless, GCMs could simulate atmospheric behavior over months or years instead of just days. That meant scientists could use GCMs to carry out climate "experiments." For example, scientists could change atmospheric CO_2 levels in

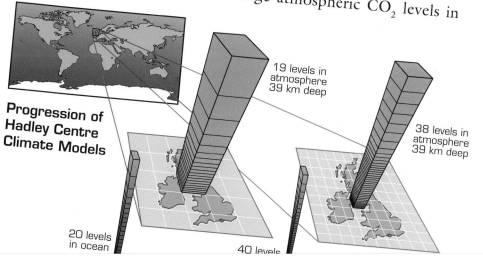

Progression of Hadley Centre Climate Models

19 levels in atmosphere 39 km deep

38 levels in atmosphere 39 km deep

20 levels in ocean

40 levels

the models and show how global surface temperature would change. Temperature changes, in turn, would alter climate over time. These climate modeling experiments produced the first climate projections. Climate projections are climate model predictions of future climate changes, based on the best available data. At last scientists had a tool for showing how increases in greenhouse gases could warm the Earth and how global warming could affect Earth's climate.

OTHER GREENHOUSE GASES

Global warming concerns began with CO_2. But scientists soon discovered that other gases could contribute to global warming.

In the 1970s, Veerabhadran Ramanathan and other scientists at the National Aeronautics and Space Administration (NASA) were studying chlorofluorocarbons (CFCs). CFCs are human-made gases. At that time, many manufacturers were using CFCs as propellants to expel the contents of spray cans and as coolants in refrigerators and air conditioners. CFCs rise easily into the atmosphere, where they stay for about one hundred years. Ramanathan reported that CFCs absorb heat ten thousand times better than CO_2 does.

Other scientists raised concerns about methane and nitrous oxide as powerful greenhouse gases. Methane comes mainly from natural processes. Cows belch methane as they digest their food. Bacteria that break down dead plants and animals release methane. Landfills release methane. So do clearing forests, burning fossil fuels, and farming many crops—especially rice. Nitrous oxide comes from burning fossil fuels, using nitrogen fertilizers, and various industrial processes. By the 1980s, scientists knew these gases, like CO_2, were on the rise.

BETTER CLIMATE MODELS

With each passing year, climate models improved. In the 1980s, climate scientists developed ocean circulation models. These models simulated many climate-related ocean processes. Eventually, researchers linked atmospheric and oceanic climate models. These atmosphere-ocean general circulation models (AOGCMs) reflected Earth's climate system far better than earlier models. AOGCMs helped scientists make climate projections more confidently.

The improved models predicted that if atmospheric CO_2 continued to increase steadily, Earth would experience several degrees of warming within a hundred years. The warming would vary by region. Higher latitudes, especially near the poles, would warm the most. The models also forecasted that glaciers and ice sheets would melt, sea levels would rise, and weather patterns worldwide would grow more unpredictable.

SCIENTISTS SPEAK OUT

Continued measurements of atmospheric CO_2 showed that by the mid-1980s, CO_2 concentration had reached 345 ppm. Measurements of global average surface temperature showed that it too was rising. Glaciers were melting faster than ever. Sea levels were a little higher. In some parts of the world, people began noticing that summ

still is) one of the most outspoken. He'd been warning government officials for several years that global warming was a serious issue. But no one seemed to be listening.

Then, during the summer of 1988, the United States suffered one of the worst heat waves on record. In the midst of it, Hansen testified before Congress about global warming. Other climate scientists supported him. This time, people paid attention. Reports on global warming soon appeared in newspapers and on television. Ordinary people began to talk about it.

CLIMATE CONTROVERSY

Still, many people—including a few prominent scientists—dismissed climate projections. Some said climate models weren't reliable or that global temperature measurements were flawed. Others felt the paleoclimatic record was too full of gaps. Many claimed that evidence of a link between CO_2 and warming was incomplete. A few skeptics claimed the mid-1900s cooling proved that increasing atmospheric CO_2 wasn't affecting Earth. Changes in Earth's surface temperature, they declared, were all part of natural climate trends. Earth's climate had changed naturally many times before. Who could say for sure that recent warming wasn't more of the same?

Global warming and climate change became a very controversial topic. People in the United States and many other countries were strongly divided on the issue. Most politicians denied the problem. They assured people there was no need to change their actions—at least not until all the facts were in.

Climate scientists realized that they needed a new way to convince the world about global warming and its potential effects on climate. In 1988 the World Meteorological Organization (WMO) and the United Nations Environment Programme (UNEP) established the Intergovernmental Panel on Climate Change (IPCC).

The IPCC studies vast amounts of climate research and evaluates the risk of climate change. The IPCC consists of three "working groups." Each group includes hundreds of climate scientists from many different countries.

For two years, the IPCC working groups reviewed thousands of scientific studies. In 1990 the IPCC released its first comprehensive report on global warming and climate change.

FROM CONTROVERSY TO CONSENSUS

The 1990 IPCC report said that human activities were substantially increasing atmospheric CO_2, methane, CFCs, and nitrous oxide. Global average surface temperature had risen 0.5° to 1.1°F (0.3° to 0.6°C) since 1890. This warming matched many earlier climate projections. But the report concluded that the warming's cause was still unclear. It could be natural climate forces, human activities, or both. There were too many uncertainties to say for sure. Scientists needed to gather more data about greenhouse gases, clouds, the oceans, and polar ice sheets before they could reach firm conclusions.

Scientists intensified their study of Earth's climate. They launched new satellites wit

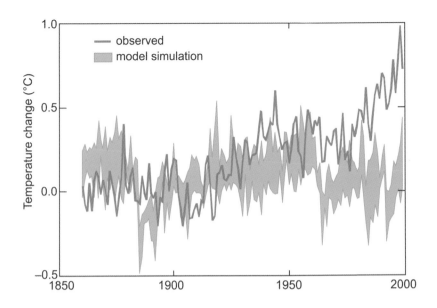

These two graphs from the Hadley Centre show that natural climate-changing forces alone can't account for recent global warming. In the top graph, climate models ran using only data on natural climate-changing forces, such as volcanic eruptions. Notice that model projections (thick green line) don't match the observed temperatures (thin red line). In the bottom graph, the same models ran using data on both natural climate-changing forces and human activities, such as burning fossil fuel. When models include the human factor, projections closely match the observed global temperatures.

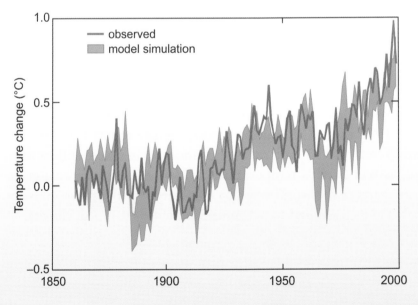

In 2001 the IPCC issued a third climate report. Nearly all the world's climate experts agreed. They believed human activities had caused Earth's recent warming. They believed further warming was inevitable. They also believed that warming, in turn, was changing Earth's climate. In some cases, dramatic change was already under way.

The IPCC released its fourth climate report in 2007. Twelve hundred climate experts from 113 countries had spent six years reviewing all the available climate research. They summarized their findings in no uncertain terms:

- Eleven of the twelve years from 1995 to 2007 ranked among the hottest years since 1860, when global surface temperature records began. The 1990s may have been the warmest decade in the past one million years.
- Global surface temperature climbed 1.4°F (0.8°C) since 1900. The rate of increase noticeably accelerated beginning in the 1980s.
- Global atmospheric CO_2 has steadily increased from 280 ppm in preindustrial times to more than 380 ppm. It shows no sign of slowing down. Ice core data show that the current CO_2 concentration is higher than at any time in the past eight hundred thousand years.
- Fossil fuel burning has caused 78 percent of the atmo-

CHAPTER THREE

MELTING ICE
AND RISING SEAS

If temperatures exceed 1.9° to 4.6°C [3.4° to 8.3°F] above preindustrial temperatures . . . eventually we would expect the Greenland ice sheet to melt. That would raise sea level by 7 meters [23 feet].
—Susan Solomon, in "Blame for Global Warming Placed Firmly on Humankind"

The IPCC's fourth report in 2007 silenced most global warming skeptics. It confirmed that fossil fuel use is increasing atmospheric carbon dioxide. It also confirmed that accumulating CO_2 is intensifying the greenhouse effect and warming Earth. Climate scientists had been right about these key issues. They had firmly established the human cause of global warming.

Is Earth's climate changing as models have predicted? The IPCC's fourth report noted evid on every continent. The data they gather help them evaluate climate models and make more accurate predictions. The information also helps people worldwide understand just how the planet is changing.

How will Earth's climate change next year? In the next decade? And in the next century? By studying current changes, scientists can better predict future ones. Their research may also reveal ways to lessen the impact of climate change. Scientists know that human actions in the next few years will set Earth's climate course far into the future.

VANISHING ARCTIC SEA ICE

Early climate models projected the greatest warming would occur at high latitudes. Later climate models agreed. Scientists have long expected polar temperatures to rise higher and faster than temperatures elsewhere on Earth.

So what's really happening at the poles? Climate scientists have been studying these regions for several decades. The evidence they've gathered confirms climate projections. Polar regions are warming at two or three times the global average rate. The Arctic is one of the world's fastest-warming places.

The Arctic is the region that surrounds the North Pole. Most of this region's land, fringing the Arctic Ocean, is flat and treeless. Much of the soil is frozen year-round.

Historically, sea ice has covered the Arctic Ocean's frigid waters. This floating ice crust can be several feet to many feet thick. But global warming is transforming it. The world has warmed an average of 1.4°F (0.8°C) since about 1900, but parts of the Arctic have warmed 4° to 5°F (2.2° to 2.8°C) just since the 1950s. As a result, Arctic sea ice is melting.

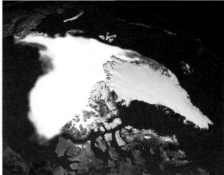

These images, based on satellite data, show recent changes in Arctic sea ice. The image on the left shows the sea ice area in summer 1979. The image on the right shows the sea ice area in summer 2007.

Scientists monitor Arctic sea ice largely from space. Satellites have captured images of Arctic sea ice continuously since 1978. These images show that the area of the ice has shrunk during that time.

Sea ice shrinking has sped up dramatically since about 2000. The worst year so far was 2007. In the summer of 2007, Arctic sea ice melted to cover just 1.65 million square miles (4.27 million sq. km). That area may seem big. But it's the smallest sea ice area in recorded history.

As sea ice melts, it leads to more Arctic warming. Arctic sea water is exposed with

In 2007 new data led scientists to revise that projection. The latest models show that Arctic sea ice could vanish by summer 2013. Wieslaw Maslowski, the head of an international research team that's modeling sea ice area loss, thinks the ice may be gone even sooner. Peter Wadhams, an expert on Arctic sea ice thickness, agrees. Wadhams used data gathered by submarines to show that the ice is thinning far faster than expected.

To confirm satellite and submarine data, researchers also gather surface data. Traveling across floating, shifting sea ice in frigid weather is a dangerous task. In 2007 the European Space Agency (ESA) enlisted two Belgian explorers to take measurements on the Arctic sea ice.

Alain Hubert and Dixie Dansercoer walked 1,240 miles (1,996 km) across the ice from Russia to Greenland. They recorded how the sea ice was melting, thinning, and breaking up all along the way. This information will help scientists assess how well existing climate models predict sea ice conditions and the rate of melting. It will also help scientists better understand data gathered by a new satellite, ESA's *CryoSat-2*.

Scientists have good evidence that global warming is melting Arctic ice shelves as well as sea ice. Ice shelves form where glaciers or ice sheets flow off land onto the ocean's surface. They are thick, floating ice platforms.

Before 2003 the Ward Hunt Ice Shelf was the largest ice shelf in the Arctic. It hugged the north coast of Canada's Ellesmere Island for at least three thousand years. Rising temperatures caused the ice shelf to melt and crack in 2000. In 2003 it split in two. Satellites captured images of the breakup. Scientists from Université Laval in Quebec, Canada, and from the University of Alaska–Fairbanks witnessed the event firsthand. They were camped on the ice shelf, gathering data.

Rivers of meltwater cover the surface of the ...

POLAR BEARS AT RISK

Melting Arctic sea ice is a major problem for polar bears. Polar bears eat seals. They hunt seals from sea ice that's fairly close to land.

During the short Arctic summer, the edge of the sea ice melts away from the land. Until recently, the ice was always close enough to land that polar bears could swim to it from land. But at least since 2000, Arctic sea ice has begun melting more than a month earlier each spring. With a longer warm season, the ice retreats much farther from land. By midsummer the sea ice may be up to 200 miles (322 km) away.

As sea ice retreats, polar bears must swim farther to reach it. Bears are strong swimmers. But they have their limits. Scientists have discovered that some polar bears drown trying to reach faraway sea ice. Others starve, unable to catch the seals they need to survive.

As Arctic warming intensifies, the risk to polar bears grows. In December 2006, the U.S. Fish and Wildlife Service proposed putting polar bears on the endangered species list.

THE GREENLAND ICE SHEET

Greenland is the world's largest island. It lies between the Arctic and Atlantic Oceans. A huge ice sheet covers about 80 percent of Greenland. Around the edges of the ice sheet, large glaciers extend like icy fingers, touching the sea along the Greenland coast.

Air temperature above Greenland has risen about 7°F (3.9°C) since the early 1990s. That warming has triggered extensive melting of Greenland's ice sheet. Scientists had expected the massive sheet to respond relatively slowly to global warming. But like Arctic sea ice, Greenland's ice sheet is melting faster than climate models projected.

Greenland has become a site of intense climate research. Science camps dot the ice sheet. Instruments measure temperature, snowfall, and ice thickness. Orbiting satellites provide a big-picture view.

Climatologist Konrad Steffen has worked on the Greenland ice sheet every year since 1990. He is with the Cooperative Institute for Research in Environmental Sciences (CIRES) in Boulder, Colorado. In 2006 his research team calculated that Greenland was losing roughly 165 billion tons (150 billion metric tons) of ice per year. That's twice as much ice as all the glaciers in the Alps (Europe's largest mountain range). "We realized something was going wrong," Steffen said. "Greenland was coming apart."

Why does this matter? All glaciers and ice sheets move. Typically, they move very slowly downhill. The Greenland ice sheet and the glaciers at its edges are moving faster than usual. They're moving faster because the meltwater beneath them lets them slide more easily over the ground. The more the ice sheet melts, the more meltwater collects beneath the ice, and the faster it moves toward the sea.

Two of eastern Greenland's largest glaciers are moving especially fast. Both doubled their speed between 2004 and 2006. They're currently moving toward the ocean at about 8.5 miles (13.7 km) per year. Scientists believe that if these glaciers are speeding toward the ocean, other Greenland glaciers probably are too.

ICE MELT IN ANTARCTICA

Antarctica is the huge frozen continent surrounding the South Pole. It holds an immense amount of ice. The ice's average thickness is 7,000 feet (2,134 m). In some spots, it's 15,000 feet (4,572 m) thick. (That's taller than Pikes Peak in Colorado!) Scientists estimate the volume of all that ice is about 7.2 million cubic miles (30 million cubic km)—about 90 percent of Earth's ice.

The Antarctic Peninsula juts out of the continent like a finger pointing toward South America. Large glaciers cover the peninsula. Surface air temperatures on the peninsula have risen 4.5°F (2.5°C) since the 1950s. In 2005 scientists found strong evidence that this warming is melting many glaciers. Alison Cook of the British Antarctica Survey (BAS) led one team studying this area. The team gathered two thousand aerial photographs and hundreds of satellite images of roughly

250 peninsular glaciers. The images dated from the late 1940s to the early 2000s. By comparing these images, scientists could see how the glaciers have changed over time. They discovered that 87 percent have retreated.

Huge ice shelves flank the eastern side of the Antarctic Peninsula. Global warming is melting these ice shelves too. One of them is the Larsen Ice Shelf. Small chunks of ice normally break off the edge of the shelf. But in 1995, an enormous piece called Larsen A cracked off. In 2002 a much older portion of the shelf, Larsen B, broke away. Larsen B was roughly the size of Rhode Island. It was 725 feet (221 m) thick. Scientists estimate it contained 720 billion tons (653 billion metric tons) of ice. Over the next month, Larsen B shattered into thousands of icebergs. Scientists are looking for telltale changes in the last remaining chunk of the ice shelf, Larsen C, that would indicate melting due to global warming.

What's causing this breakup? Larsen B, in particular, had survived thousands of years of climate variations. What was different about 2002? Summer 2002 was one of the Antarctic Peninsula's warmest summers on record. Ted Scambos of the National Snow and Ice Data Center (NSIDC) at the University of Colorado is one of many researchers who studied the Larsen Ice Shelf breakup. He and other scientists think warmer temperatures were a major factor. Melting ice formed pools of meltwater on the ice shelf's surface. This water melted the ice below it, causing it to crack. When the cracks grew large enough, the weakened ice gave way.

The Antarctic Peninsula's ice is only a fraction of the continent's total ice. Most of Antarctica's ice is in two vast ice sheets. The smaller one covers West Antarctica. The larger one covers East Antarctica. The Antarctic interior is much colder than the peninsula. The heart of the East Antarctic ice sheet is the coldest place on Earth.

Climate models originally predicted it would take hundreds of years for evidence of global warming to appear in Antarctica's interior. But the models were too conservative. Global warming has reached this frigid place already.

In 2005 NASA scientists studying satellite images of West Antarctica found a surprise. They spotted large pools of meltwater about 311 miles (500 km) from the South Pole. This was the first sign of significant warming in Antarctica's bitterly cold interior. In 2006 scientists found more signs of melting. Some researchers think that the West Antarctic ice sheet may be in the very early stages of disintegrating. Other scientists say different factors may be involved. They need much more evidence to know for sure what's happening to the ice.

The East Antarctic ice sheet still seems relatively stable. It's much larger and thicker than the West Antarctic ice sheet. It's the coldest mass of ice on Earth. Scientists have observed changes even here. They just aren't quite sure how to interpret the changes yet. Near the center of the ice sheet, close to the South Pole, average temperatures have actually dropped slightly since about 1980. The edges of the ice sheet, however, show some evidence of possible warming. In 2007 Australian researchers reported that the top of Tottenham Glacier near the East Antarctic coast has melted down by 33 feet (10 m) since the early 1990s.

MOUNTAIN GLACIERS

Glaciers nestle among the peaks of the world's highest mountain ranges. Bruce Molnia and other researchers have documented dramatic glacier retreat in Alaska. Scientists have found similar evidence of glacial melting in many other parts of the world too.

Since 1850 glaciers in the European Alps have shrunk 30 to 40 percent. Southern New Zealand's mountain glaciers have shrunk at least 25 percent since the early 1900s. They've decreased by almost 11 percent since the 1980s. The Tasman Glacier, New Zealand's longest, has retreated several miles in that time.

Since the 1950s, Himalayan mountain glaciers have also been shrinking. Stretching across central Asia, the Himalayas have nearly fifteen thousand glaciers, more than any other nonpolar region. Climate models predict that because of global warming, 80 percent of Himalayan glaciers will likely disappear by 2100.

Glacial geologist Lonnie Thompson, from Ohio State University's Byrd Polar Research Center (BPRC), is a leading expert on climate change and mountain glaciers. Thompson has trekked up hundreds of mountains on all seven continents. During his scientific career, he has led nearly fifty expeditions to study mountain glaciers.

Many of those glaciers are on high mountains in tropical regions of the world (near the equator). Evidence gathered by Thompson and other glacier experts shows that tropical glaciers are melting rapidly. And their melting rate is increasing over time. On one glacier in the Andes Mountains of Peru, melting was thirty-two times greater between 1999 and 2001 than it was between 1963 and 1978. Thompson and his colleagues predict that most tropical mountain glaciers will likely disappear by 2050, if not sooner. "These glaciers are very much like the canaries once used in coal mines," Thompson said. "They're an indicator of massive changes taking place and a response to the changes in climate in the tropics."

Not all mountain glaciers are retreating. In a few places, higher temperatures are causing more snowfall on mountain peaks. (Warmer air can hold more moisture than colder air.) Where it's snowing more, some glaciers are growing slightly. But if global temperatures keep rising, scientists suspect melting will overcome snowfall in these places. Climate models project that if global average temperature rises 7.2°F (4°C), all the world's mountain glaciers will melt.

SEA LEVEL RISE

Sea level is a measure of ocean water volume. Sea level measurements show how high onto land the ocean reaches. All climate models project that global warming will raise sea level.

Sea level can rise in three ways. The first is thermal expansion. When water warms, water molecules spread out and take up more space. As global warming heats the upper layers of the ocean, the warmed water expands and climbs higher onto land.

Sea level can also rise when water is added to the oceans. When ice sheets and glaciers melt, their water moves from land to ocean. The added water raises sea level.

Finally, sea level can rise when seawater grows less salty. Freshwater, which contains little or no salt, is less dense than salt water. Freshwater takes up slightly more space than an equal mass of salt water. So when fresh glacial meltwater flows into the ocean, it makes the ocean less salty and raises sea level.

Sea level has risen and fallen many times during Earth's long history. The peak of the last major glaciation was about eighteen thousand years ago. As Earth's climate warmed and glaciers

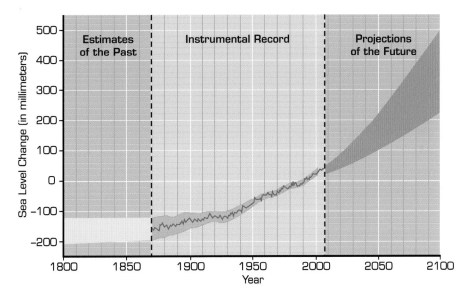

Sea level has risen steadily since the mid-1800s. Using current evidence, models project sea level will keep rising as increasing global temperatures continue to warm ocean waters and melt glaciers and ice sheets.

melted, sea level rose about 400 feet (122 m). Most of that increase happened more than six thousand years ago. After that, sea level rose only slightly. In fact, from roughly three thousand years ago to the year 1800, sea level remained almost unchanged. But in the mid-1800s, sea level began rising slightly.

Sea level measurements used to come mostly from tide gauges. These instruments are set up along coastlines. They measure sea level by monitoring tides and waves. Since 1992 satellites have measured sea level from space too. One of the first to do so was *TOPEX/Poseidon. Jason-1* eventually took its place. Scientists also began using ocean floats (instruments that drift in the ocean) to gather sea level data. More accurate tools gave scientists a clearer picture of sea level changes worldwide. Between 1993 and 2005, sea level rose an average of 0.1 inches (3 millimeters) per year. Scientists estimate that about half that increase came from thermal expansion. The other half came from glacial meltwater. Scientists also note a troubling aspect of these measurements: the rate of sea level rise accelerated during the last few years of the 1900s.

In 2002 scientists gained another useful tool for studying both oceans and ice. NASA launched twin satellites that form the Gravity Recovery and Climate Experiment (GRACE). GRACE precisely measures surface height of the ocean worldwide. It also measures the sizes of large glaciers and ice sheets. In other words, GRACE can measure melting ice and sea level rise at the same time. For example, GRACE data showed that between 2002 and 2005, melting Antarctic ice alone raised global sea level 0.06 inches (1.5 mm).

In 2008 NASA will launch a new satellite, *Jason-2*. It will gather detailed information about 95 percent of the world's ice-free ocean every ten days. Coupling sea surface height measurements with other data will help scientists improve climate model projections of future sea level rise.

More accurate projections are vital because the range of possibilities is so wide. Current models project that global warming will trigger significant sea level rise during the twenty-first century. But how high the ocean will rise is still very uncertain. It depends on how much land ice melts and flows into the sea.

If all the world's glaciers melt, for example, scientists estimate their combined water will raise sea level about 1.6 feet (0.5 m). If the entire Greenland ice sheet melts, it will raise sea level another 24 feet (7.3 m). Melting of the West Antarctic ice sheet would raise sea level an additional 20 feet (6 m). If all the ice in Antarctica melts, that 20-foot increase would jump to 200 feet (61 m).

A total global ice meltdown is unlikely. But it's not impossible. The current rate of sea level rise is already at the high end of climate projections. Many scientists worry that glaciers and ice sheets are melting far faster than expected. If they are, then sea level may rise faster than expected too.

Even a small sea level rise could be disastrous. Rising seas are already affecting small islands. The tiny Pacific nation of Tuvalu consists of nine low-lying coral islands. Tuvalu's highest point is only 13 feet (4 m) above sea level. Rising seas are submerging the islands' beaches. Several other island nations, including the Maldives in the Indian Ocean and the Marshall Islands in the Pacific, could disappear within this century. Most of the people on these islands live very close to sea level. A rise of just 3 feet (1 m) would be devastating. Long before the water climbs that high, salt water would invade the islands' freshwater supplies, making the water undrinkable.

Two percent of Earth's land is lower than 33 feet (10 m) above sea level. But that land is home to 10 percent of Earth's people. A 16.5-foot (5 m) increase in sea level would submerge large parts of the world's major coastal cities. New York, London, Sydney, Vancouver, Mumbai, Shanghai, and Tokyo would all be largely underwater. In Florida, Louisiana, and countries such as the Netherlands and Bangladesh, entire regions would vanish. Roughly 650 million people would have to move to higher ground.

THE WARMING OCEAN

Large bodies of water can absorb a great deal of heat. The ocean is the world's largest heat sink. (A heat sink is an environment or object that absorbs and disperses heat from another environment or object.) Ocean waters absorb heat from solar energy and from the air. Ocean currents carry this heat around the globe. In this way, the ocean helps stabilize global temperatures. It plays a vital role in Earth's climate system.

Global warming is raising the air temperature above Earth's surface. But is global warming also raising ocean temperature? If so, how will that affect ocean ecosystems? How will it affect climate worldwide?

Answering these questions isn't easy. Imagine trying to measure the temperature of water that covers 71 percent of the planet, with an average depth of 12,500 feet (3,810 m)! But scientists are meeting the challenge.

Researchers measure the ocean's surface temperature from ships. Instruments on floating buoys collect similar data. Satellites measure sea surface temperature too. Data from all these instruments show that parts of the ocean's surface are warming as global temperature rises. But what about deeper water?

To monitor deeper ocean waters, scientists developed the Argo program in 2000. Argo is a global array of more than three thousand freely drifting ocean floats. Argo floats don't just bob on the surface. They also dive. An Argo float can dive about 1.2 miles (2 km). Sensors inside the float measure temperature, salinity (saltiness), and other water characteristics all the way down. They relay that data almost instantly to receiving stations around the world.

The Japan Coast Guard is about to pick up this Argo float, which measures ocean water temperature and other characteristics.

Argo floats, satellites, and other instruments have given scientists a reasonably accurate picture of ocean temperature. Since the early 1960s, Earth's oceans have warmed 0.18°F (0.10°C) from the surface to a depth of 2,310 feet (704 m). That may not seem like much. But raising the temperature of an entire ocean—even a fraction of a degree—takes a huge amount of heat energy.

Is ocean warming a result of greenhouse gases and global warming? Yes, according to a 2005 report by scientists from Scripps Institution of Oceanography and the Lawrence Livermore National Laboratory in California. Marine physicist Tim Barnett and climatologist David Pierce compiled ocean temperature measurements dating back to the 1970s. They compared the measurements to climate projections. Models had predicted that increasing greenhouse gases should cause ocean heating. The temperature data matched the projections. "We were stunned by the degree of similarity between the observations and the models," said Barnett.

Ocean warming isn't uniform all over the world or from surface to floor. Scientists know that shallow waters warm faster than deeper ones. And climate models projected that tropical oceans would warm the most. Recent data show that again, the models were right. Tropical waters have indeed been warming since the 1950s, at a faster rate than polar waters.

Has ocean warming affected Earth's climate? Scientists have found some links between tropical ocean warming and climate changes in the Northern Hemisphere. North American winters have grown warmer and wetter as oceans have warmed. In northern Europe, climate has become wetter and milder. In southern Europe and the Middle East, however, conditions have grown drier.

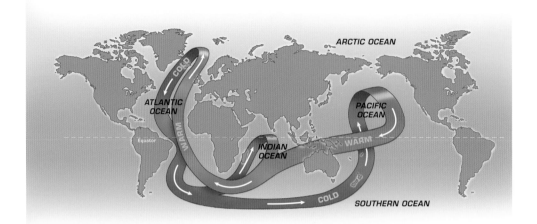

Earth's deep ocean currents distribute heat around the planet in a predictable way. Global warming may change how these currents move.

OCEAN CIRCULATION

Rising ocean temperature may affect climate in another important way. It could change the way ocean currents flow. The wind generally drives surface currents. But currents also flow far below the surface. These deep ocean currents move around the planet in a specific pattern. Density differences in ocean water drive these currents. Density, in turn, is a product of temperature and salinity.

Scientists call Earth's pattern of deep ocean currents thermohaline circulation. *Thermo* refers to temperature, while *haline* refers to saltiness. A common term for thermohaline circulation is the great ocean conveyor belt. Like a conveyor belt, deep ocean currents swirl around the continents, carrying heat as they go.

Thermohaline circulation starts in the Arctic. Ocean water near the North Pole gets very cold. The surface of the water freezes, forming sea ice. The freezing process leaves salt behind, making the water under the ice saltier. This increases the water's density, and it sinks. Surface water moves in to replace the sinking water.

The deep current of cold water moves south through the Atlantic Ocean and toward the tips of Africa and South America. It sweeps past Antarctica, where the water cools even more and sinks even deeper. From the Southern Ocean, the current heads north into the Indian and Pacific oceans. It warms as it nears the equator. This warmer water rises. Then it loops southward and westward into the South Atlantic. Eventually it heads north, where the cycle begins again.

The great ocean conveyor belt affects the climates of islands and continents it passes. For example, a part of the conveyor belt is a warm current called the Gulf Stream. One arm of this current, called the North Atlantic Drift, carries warm water across the northern Atlantic Ocean. It keeps northern Europe warmer than other regions at the same latitude.

Recent studies suggest that global warming may be affecting thermohaline circulation. In the Arctic, huge amounts of relatively warm freshwater are entering the ocean. This water comes from melting sea ice and Greenland's melting glaciers and ice sheet. This influx of warm freshwater may disrupt the sinking of cold salt water. This change, in turn, could slow or even stop the conveyor belt.

In 2006 a research team found evidence that the North Atlantic Drift may be weakening. Other scientists have yet to confirm this. If thermohaline circulation ever does slow down or stop, it could drastically change the climate in many parts of the world.

CHAPTER FOUR

ALTERED ECOSYSTEMS, ENDANGERED SPECIES, AND EXTREME WEATHER

If we do not slow down the rate of global warming, many species are likely to become extinct. In effect we are pushing them off the planet.

—James E. Hansen, in "NASA Study Finds World Warmth Edging Ancient Levels"

Scientists have gathered conclusive evidence that global warming is melting sea ice, glaciers, and ice sheets. Fresh meltwater and thermal expansion are raising sea level. Global warming is directly warming the ocean too. It may change how ocean currents move around the planet and influence Earth's climate.

These findings are only the beginning. Climate models have long predicted that global warming would directly change many aspects of the climate worldwide. And sure enough, scientists are discovering evidence of sweeping climate change. They're finding it near the poles, along the equator, and at all latitudes in between.

Climate change is altering habitats around the world. This monkey is just one of the many animals in South America's Amazon rain forest that may face extinction because of climate change.

THE THAWING TUNDRA

Even the earliest climate models indicated that global warming would be more severe near the poles. Later models gave the same projection. All were correct. Polar regions are warming two to three times faster than equatorial regions. In the Arctic, rising surface air temperatures are not just melting ice. They're also melting a frozen land.

The Arctic tundra lies south of the Arctic Ocean. It is a flat, treeless landscape. Only small plants such as shrubs, grasses, mosses, and lichens can survive the tundra's long, dark, bitterly cold winters. During the brief Arctic summer, the top few inches of frozen soil thaw. Shallow ponds and lakes form. Below all that, the ground stays frozen. This ever-frozen soil is called permafrost.

The climate of the Arctic tundra is changing. Winters aren't as cold as they used to be. Spring starts earlier. Summer is warmer and longer. This warmer climate is profoundly changing the tundra ecosystem. Instead of small summertime ponds, large lakes are forming. Bushes and trees are growing where only mosses and lichens grew before. Animals never seen before on the tundra are moving in from the south. The biggest change is happening underground. Millions of square miles of permafrost are melting.

Tundra soil stores a lot of carbon. It's rich in the preserved remains of ancient plants. Scientists estimate that worldwide, permafrost holds 992 billion tons (900 billion metric tons) of carbon.

As the Arctic has warmed, this vast mass of dead, frozen plant matter has begun to thaw and decompose. When plants decompose, they release carbon dioxide into the air. Climate change on the tundra is directly adding huge amounts of CO_2

to the atmosphere. If tundra soils were to release all their carbon, atmospheric CO_2 would more than double.

Not all the tundra's carbon is entering the atmosphere as CO_2. Tundra lakes and soggy soils are home to methane-producing bacteria. Plant material decomposing in the water provides these bacteria with food. The bacteria then release vast amounts of methane. That methane is bubbling up from tundra lakes at a frightening rate.

CLIMATE TIPPING POINTS

Methane is a very potent greenhouse gas. Much more methane is coming from the thawing tundra than scientists estimated as recently as 2000. The problem is a vicious circle of warming. Global warming is thawing the tundra. The thawing tundra is releasing carbon dioxide and methane. All that atmospheric CO_2 and methane will cause more warming.

Scientists view the tundra situation as one of several climate "tipping points." Imagine walking along the top of a very thin wall. You're teetering back and forth, trying to keep your balance. One small occurrence, such as a gust of wind, could push you off. Parts of Earth's climate system may be balanced precariously like this. After months or years of gradual change, one or more of these parts may reach a critical state. Beyond that point, climate might tip. It could abruptly change in large and unexpected ways.

Some climate experts fear that the tundra's methane release may increase so much and so fast that it will cause a sudden, unexpectedly large rise in global temperatures. Other tipping points could be a sudden collapse of the West Antarctic ice sheet or a major change in thermohaline circulation.

A scientist measures the ground-level temperature on the tundra in northern Alaska. Recent ground-level warming is melting permafrost across vast expanses of Arctic tundra.

In 2005 Sergei Kirpotin of Tomsk State University in Russian Siberia and Judith Marquand of the University of Oxford in Great Britain studied permafrost in Siberia. They discovered that about 386,000 square miles (1 million sq. km) of permafrost in western Siberia is melting. Other scientists report similar permafrost melting in northern Alaska and northern Canada.

Scientists estimate that thawing permafrost is releasing methane and CO_2 five times faster than climate models have predicted. The western Siberian tundra alone could release 70 billion tons (64 billion metric tons) of methane into the air. As a greenhouse gas, methane is twenty-three times better than CO_2 at trapping heat in the atmosphere.

CLIMATE ZONES ON THE MOVE

As Earth warms, climate models project that its major climate zones will shift. Winters are already warmer in many parts of the Northern Hemisphere. Summers are hotter and last longer. The same is true of similar latitudes in the Southern Hemisphere. Such changes in average temperature, along with changes in precipitation (rain and snow) patterns, are the first signs of climate zone shifts.

In general, climate models show that existing climate zones will shift toward higher latitudes and higher elevations. Scientists already have clear evidence of such shifting in Arctic and subarctic regions. Trees, shrubs, and other plants that once grew south of the tundra have spread northward. On islands off the Antarctic Peninsula, populations of two native Antarctic flowering plants increased rapidly between 1964 and 1990. Once able to survive only in small sheltered spots, the plants are spreading quickly on the islands thanks to warmer summer temperatures and a longer growing season.

In the United States, trees and shrubs that once grew in the northeastern states are spreading into southeastern Canada. Trees common to southeastern states are spreading northward too.

In 2007 Daniel W. McKenney of the Canadian Forest Service and his colleagues published a detailed study of 130 North American tree species. The researchers collected records showing where these species grew in the past. They documented where each species currently grows. They used computer models to project where the species might grow in the future, as temperature and precipitation patterns change. The scientists concluded that many kinds of North American trees will likely shift their ranges northward by 435 miles (700 km). Many

Central American and South American plant species will likely move northward as well.

Researchers at the University of Wisconsin–Madison and the University of Wyoming predict that some of Earth's climate zones will disappear by the year 2100. Using climate models, the scientists studied average summer and winter temperatures and precipitation to map the differences between current climate zones and those expected in 2100. Climates currently found in tropical mountain highlands and polar regions will very likely disappear by the next century. Tropical and subtropical regions may develop completely new types of climates.

Changes in the tropics are already under way. Scientists have hard evidence that the tropical climate zone is expanding. This zone is like a belt around Earth's equator. Historically, it lay between the latitudes of 23.5° north and 23.5° south. Five different types of satellites show that since 1979, vegetation characteristic of the tropical climate zone has expanded two to five degrees of latitude on both sides of the equator. This expansion is happening much faster than climate models projected.

HEAT WAVES AND OTHER WEIRD WEATHER

As climate changes, so will weather. Models project that as Earth warms, moderate weather patterns will tip toward extreme weather patterns. Heat waves will probably happen more often. Dry spells will tend to escalate into droughts. Devastating storms will grow more common.

It's impossible to pin a single weather event on global warming. Weather varies naturally and always will. Nevertheless, almost every continent is experiencing changing weather patterns. The global nature of these changes suggests a global cause.

A small rise in a place's average temperature increases the likelihood of summer heat waves. The higher global temperature rises, the greater the chance of more frequent and more severe heat waves.

Heat waves appear to be increasing. In August 2003, Europe suffered the worst heat wave it had ever experienced. The heat claimed more than thirty-five thousand lives. Thermometers in London, England, registered temperatures over 100°F (38°C) for the first time in history.

In 2006 Europe suffered more terrible heat waves, as did the United States. In 2007 heat waves struck southeastern Europe, India, Pakistan, western and central Russia, and parts of North Africa.

Young people in Lahore, Pakistan, cool off in a canal during a June 2007 heat wave.

"It's the extremes, not the averages, that cause the most damage to society and to many ecosystems," said Claudia Tebaldi. Tebaldi is a climate scientist at the National Center for Atmospheric Research (NCAR) in Boulder, Colorado. In 2006 Tebaldi and several colleagues used nine different climate models to project weather patterns through 2099. All nine models told the same story. The world will very likely face greater risk of heat waves in this century.

FLOODS AND DROUGHTS

Climate models also agree that global warming will lead to an increase in global precipitation. This is because warmer conditions near the Earth's surface evaporate more water from oceans, lakes, and rivers. Warm air can hold more water vapor than cooler air. More water vapor in the air means more precipitation.

Global precipitation over land has already increased by roughly 1 percent since 1900. During that period, average precipitation in the United States has increased by at least 5 percent. The precipitation change hasn't been the same everywhere in the country, however. Some areas of the United States have had up to a 20 percent increase, while others have seen up to a 20 percent decrease. Why? Differences in winds, temperatures, and landforms such as mountain ranges all affect rainfall and snowfall patterns.

More water vapor in the air will likely cause more frequent heavy precipitation events. Higher temperatures in the atmosphere provide more energy for severe storms, such as large thunderstorms, to form. And those drenching, long-lasting rainstorms tend to cause floods.

In August 2007, record-breaking floods ravaged parts of the United Kingdom. The floods submerged houses, roads, crops, and pastures. Just a few months later, terrible floods hit Indonesia. In the city of Jakarta, floodwater forced thousands of people to leave their homes. The water level reached 23 feet (7 m) in the worst areas. At roughly the same time, floods hit parts of India, Bangladesh, and Nepal. The floods displaced nearly twenty million people.

To monitor precipitation worldwide, scientists are using a new satellite called Tropical Rainfall Measuring Mission (TRMM). The United States and Japan operate TRMM jointly. Before TRMM launched in 1997, scientists had no instruments that could record rainfall worldwide, especially over the ocean. TRMM is a sort of space-based rain gauge. It uses microwaves to estimate how much rain clouds are producing.

As global temperature continues to rise, scientists expect precipitation to keep rising as well. But just as different parts of the United States are growing wetter or drier, so will different regions of the world. Where warmer temperatures make more water evaporate from the land than precipitation replaces, the climate will grow drier. The warmer it gets, the drier these places will become.

Many climate models predict that during the twenty-first century, pockets of especially dry air will tend to settle over the southwestern United States, parts of Mexico, eastern Australia, and southern Africa. This especially dry air could bring prolonged droughts to these regions. "We think of drought as being an occasional thing, but it's not going to be like that in the future," said Ming Fang Ting, a scientist at Columbia University's Earth Institute. "It's going to be dry all the time" in some places.

Scientists at the Hadley Centre for Climate Prediction and Research in the United Kingdom report that about 3 percent of Earth's land is currently experiencing extreme drought.

Their climate models project that by 2100, the amount of land suffering from extreme drought will rise to 30 percent. Since 2000, the southwestern United States has seen both rising temperatures and dramatically declining precipitation. Together these factors have plunged the area into one of the worst and longest droughts on record. Since 2001 Australia has also suffered from the worst drought in its history. Some government officials say that climate change is making parts of Australia unable to sustain agriculture.

Recently, research revealed that drought does more than just dry out land. It also intensifies global warming. How? Wilting plants take up less CO_2. That leaves more of the greenhouse gas in the atmosphere.

HEAT + DROUGHT = FIRE

Where severe droughts and high temperatures meet, conditions are ideal for wildfires. Models project that global warming will raise the risk of wildfires in many parts of the world. Evidence shows that wildfires are already happening more often.

A rural firefighter watches a bushfire rage through an Australian national park in January 2007.

Scientists from the University of Arizona and the University of California–San Diego analyzed forest fire activity across the western United States since 1970. They compared that information to the region's climate data from the same period. They found that the number and intensity of large wildfires jumped in the 1980s. Compared to previous years, 1987 to 2004 saw four times as many wildfires. Those fires burned almost seven times as much land. The wildfire season in western states is about ten weeks longer than it was in 1987. This is due to warmer spring temperatures and earlier, faster melting of mountain snows.

SEVERE STORMS

Models predict that as the world warms and climate changes, severe storms—especially hurricanes—will increase. Hurricanes (also called typhoons) are large, intense, rotating wind-and-rain storms. They draw their energy from warm ocean waters. As tropical oceans grow warmer, they may spawn more and more powerful hurricanes.

Scientists have documented an increase in the number of hurricanes in the Atlantic Ocean since 1995. In 2005 the Atlantic saw four Category 5 hurricanes: Emily, Katrina, Rita, and Wilma. (A Category 5 hurricane is the most powerful and destructive type of hurricane). That was a world record for the most Category 5 hurricanes in one year. Hurricane Katrina was the most destructive hurricane in U.S. history. But was Katrina the result of global warming?

Climate scientists are divided on this question. Some say the 2005 hurricane season is evidence that warmer tropical oceans are producing more hurricanes. Other researchers disagree.

This 2006 satellite image shows Hurricane Gordon (top) and Hurricane Helene (bottom) *forming in the Atlantic Ocean.*

They say individual hurricanes, like all individual weather events, result from many factors. They claim scientists haven't collected enough clear evidence to show that global warming is the sole culprit. Other climate-shaping factors, such as El Niño events, may also be at work. Christopher Landsea, of NOAA's National Hurricane Center, points to evidence of hurricane activity cycles that last for twenty-five to forty years.

Nevertheless, other scientists have uncovered a possible link between global warming and hurricane strength. Kevin Trenberth, an NCAR hurricane expert, analyzed hurricane data from 1975 to 2005. He found that the number of strong hurricanes in both the North Atlantic and North Pacific increased during that period. Trenberth's findings correspond with a documented rise in sea surface temperatures in these waters. Peter Webster from the Georgia Institute of Technology has documented a global increase in severe (Categories 4 and 5) hurricanes in recent decades. Webster found that between 1975 and 1989, 171 severe hurricanes occurred worldwide. From 1990 to 2005, there were 269.

CHANGING SEASONS

Climate models predict that as global temperatures rise, seasons will change in many parts of the world. Scientists already have clear evidence of such change. In Europe spring begins one to two weeks earlier than it did in the 1970s. In Alaska spring arrives at least two weeks earlier than it did in the 1950s. Spring snowmelt in the Rocky Mountains occurs roughly four weeks earlier than it did in the 1950s. In many places with cold winters, lakes freeze later in the fall. They thaw earlier in the spring.

Changing seasons affect plant and animal life cycles. Scientists examined 125,000 studies of more than five hundred different European plants. Seventy-five percent of the plants bloom earlier than they did in the 1970s. They produce fruit and seeds earlier too.

Scientists note similar trends in the United States. In studies of fourteen hundred different plants and animals, more than 80 percent start their spring activities earlier than they used to. On average, trees bud, insects hatch, frogs mate, and birds lay eggs more than a week earlier than they did in the 1960s.

ANIMALS ON THE GO

Changing temperatures, seasons, and climate zones are affecting entire populations of animals. As conditions become too warm or too dry, animals move to more suitable habitats if they can. In a 2003 study, scientists showed that the populations of dozens of North American animal species shifted northward about 4 miles (6.4 km) per decade since the mid-1900s. Since the early 1980s, seven types of North American warblers have shifted their range north by more than 65 miles (105 km).

Some birds have changed the timing of their seasonal migrations. They move to summer breeding grounds earlier, to meet spring's earlier arrival. Fish are on the move too. Scientists have documented cases of at least twenty-one species of ocean fish leaving waters that have grown too warm. Some species moved to higher latitudes. Other species moved to deeper water.

Scientists have evidence of a massive ecological shift in the northern Bering Sea. (The Bering Sea is the northernmost part of the Pacific Ocean.) Water temperatures there have risen 5.4°F (3°C) since the 1970s. Walruses, bearded seals, and gray whales used to spend many months feeding in the Bering Sea each year. These species are becoming rare in the Bering Sea.

They've moved north into the cooler Arctic Ocean. At the same time, fish species common farther south in the Pacific are turning up in the Bering Sea.

CHANGING ECOSYSTEMS

Entire ecosystems are changing as Earth warms up. Some, such as the Arctic tundra, are already disappearing. Ecosystems elsewhere are changing too.

In shallow equatorial waters, rising ocean temperatures are killing corals. Corals are tiny sea animals that often live in colonies. Together, the hard outer shells of these coral colonies form massive underwater formations called coral reefs. Coral reefs provide habitat for thousands of ocean species, including sea stars, anemones, and countless colorful tropical fish.

Most reef-building corals contain microscopic algae. These algae carry out photosynthesis to make food for themselves and their coral hosts. Unusually warm water can cause coral to expel their algae. This loss is called coral bleaching because it turns

The contrast between bleached coral (left) and healthy coral (right) is obvious in this photo taken on a coral reef near a tropical island in the Pacific Ocean.

the corals white. A temperature increase of just 1.8°F (1°C) can bleach corals. Bleached corals can recover. If the water cools soon, algae can grow inside the corals again. But without their algae, corals slowly starve.

Over the past one hundred years, surface temperature has been rising in many tropical seas. Before the 1980s, seawater was still generally cool enough that coral bleaching was rare. When bleaching did occur, corals usually recovered. But tropical ocean temperatures have risen more sharply since then. Coral bleaching has become much more common. In 1998 temperatures spiked. Coral reefs around the world experienced the worst bleaching in recorded history. Sixty countries in and near the Pacific Ocean, Indian Ocean, Red Sea, Persian Gulf, Mediterranean Sea, and Caribbean Sea reported coral bleaching. Australia's Great Barrier Reef, the largest reef system in the world, was hit hard. But Indian Ocean corals suffered the most. More than 70 percent of them died.

In 2002 an even worse bleaching occurred. It affected massive areas of corals all over the world. Nearly 60 percent of the coral on the Great Barrier Reef bleached. In the worst areas, 90 percent of the coral turned white.

Marine biologists from the Australian Institute of Marine Science collected data showing that 2002 was the warmest year since 1870 on the Great Barrier Reef. Scientists worldwide worry that rising ocean temperatures may destroy most of the world's coral reefs in the next few decades.

South America's vast Amazon rain forest is the largest tropical forest on Earth. This ecosystem is home to more species of plants and animals than any other region on the planet. But conditions in the Amazon are changing.

In 2005 and 2006, severe drought struck much of the Amazon region. Scientists suspect warmer Atlantic waters reduced the moisture available to this region. Furthermore, people cut and burn thousands of acres of rain forest each year. People clear the forest mostly to open up land for farming and ranching. But clearing also opens up large patches of land to the sun's hot rays. This exposure contributes to the forest's overall drying.

Researchers studying the Amazon rain forest worry that continued drought could eventually kill large numbers of trees. A combination of drought and deforestation (clearing) could push the Amazon past its tipping point. Much—if not all—of the forest might vanish. So might most of its plants and animals.

In 2007 scientists realized that the ecosystems at greatest risk may be those in the ocean. As Revelle and Suess discovered, surface waters become saturated with (unable to hold more) CO_2 and start releasing the gas back to the atmosphere. But deep ocean currents gradually bring water not saturated with

THE AMAZON AND CO_2

Plants in the Amazon rain forest take in a lot of CO_2 during photosynthesis. The carbon in that CO_2 ends up in trunks, branches, stems, vines, and leaves. In this way, the forest serves as a huge carbon reservoir.

If drought kills Amazon trees, they'll stop taking CO_2 from the air. The dead trees would also create an extreme risk of forest fires. Fires would release huge amounts of CO_2 into the atmosphere.

Loss of the Amazon rain forest would be a global catastrophe. Scientists estimate the forest contains 90 billion tons (82 billion metric tons) of carbon. That's enough to increase the rate of global warming by 50 percent.

CO_2 to the surface. As a result, the ocean is slowly absorbing CO_2 (although not nearly as much as human activities are adding to the atmosphere).

As the ocean absorbs CO_2, seawater is gradually becoming more acidic. The ocean is already 30 percent more acidic than it was at the beginning of the Industrial Revolution. It's absorbing roughly 22 tons (20 metric tons) of CO_2 every day. And some oceanographers fear the change might be irreversible.

Ocean acidification could be very damaging. Acid destroys shells. Many sea animals, such as oysters, clams, and crabs, have shells. So do krill (tiny shrimplike animals) and many of the animals in plankton (a variety of drifting, microscopic sea organisms).

Krill and plankton form the base of most ocean food chains. They are food for many kinds of fish and some sea mammals. Without their shells, krill and many of the animals in plankton would die. So would everything that depends on them for survival. "When you start messing with the lower end of the food chain, it can dramatically affect the higher end of the food chain," said Richard Feely, an oceanographer with NOAA.

VANISHING SPECIES

Shifting climate zones and seasons may endanger many of Earth's living things. Organisms that can adapt quickly to environmental changes may survive. Those that can't adapt will probably go extinct (die out).

In 2003 Camille Parmesan, a biologist at the University of Texas, published an extensive report about global warming's effects on living things worldwide. Parmesan compiled data from more than eight hundred scientific studies on thousands of species. She found that very adaptable species are surviving global warming—so far. Edith's checkerspot butterfly, for example, has adapted by moving. Its population is declining sharply near the Mexico-California border. Conditions there have become too warm and dry for the butterfly. So it has moved hundreds of miles north into Canada. Just a few decades ago, Canada's climate would have been too cold for this butterfly. But it's thriving there.

"[S]pecies that are adapted to a wide array of environments...will be most likely to persist," said Parmesan. She found that many less-adaptable species are not faring so well. Parmesan concluded that climate change has already caused extinctions in some ecosystems. Many species are seriously endangered. Species living in the fastest-changing ecosystems face the greatest risk.

In 2004 a large international team of scientists studied six very biodiverse regions around the world. (A very biodiverse place is home to many different kinds of living things.) The scientists used computer models to simulate the ways species' ranges may react to global warming and climate change. Using the models, the scientists projected the future ranges of 1,103 plants, mammals, birds, reptiles, frogs, butterflies, and more.

The results? Between 15 and 37 percent of all species in the regions studied could go extinct before 2050. The scientists believe that extinctions due to climate change are also probable elsewhere. Chris Thomas of Great Britain's University of Leeds, who led the team, summed up their findings. "If the projections can be extrapolated globally, and to other groups of land animals and plants," he reported, "our analyses suggest that well over a million species could be threatened with extinction as a result of climate change."

CHAPTER FIVE

THE CHALLENGE OF A WARMER WORLD

I believe we will rise to this challenge. But we have to start very quickly, and we have to make it our priority.

—Nobel Prize winner, Al Gore

In November 2007, United Nations secretary-general Ban Ki-moon announced the release of the final version of the IPCC's fourth report on climate change. "Today the world's scientists have spoken clearly," he said, "and with one voice."

Hundreds of leading climate scientists had studied decades of climate data. They'd analyzed information gathered from the ocean floor to the upper atmosphere. Their conclusion was firm: human activities that emit greenhouse gases into the atmosphere have caused most of the rise in global average temperature since at least the mid-1900s.

Furthermore, scientists had gathered overwhelming evidence showing the impact of global warming on Earth's climate. That evidence revealed a world in which temperatures are warming,

Extreme heat waves that struck Pakistan in May 2007 caused droughts that forced rural women to travel long distances for water.

weather is more severe, climate zones are changing, snow and ice are melting, and sea level is rising.

LOOKING AHEAD

What do these changes mean for Earth's future? How will they affect plants, animals, and people? Climate projections have been remarkably accurate so far. The latest climate models give a reasonably clear and reliable picture of what probably lies ahead.

All climate models agree that global warming will intensify in the coming years. Fossil fuels power modern societies. People won't stop using them overnight. Carbon dioxide and other greenhouse gases will keep collecting in the atmosphere. Even if greenhouse gas emissions ended immediately, Earth would still warm several degrees. That's because greenhouse gases already in the atmosphere will stay there for decades.

Just how much Earth will warm is still an open question. People can control the rate of greenhouse gas accumulation. By reducing greenhouse gas emissions, humans may be able to slow future warming.

SIX DIFFERENT FUTURES

The scientists who created the IPCC's fourth report used more than a dozen of the latest climate models to project warming by the 2090s. The report offers six different projections for six different emissions scenarios. The scenarios reflect varying concentrations of atmospheric CO_2.

The best-case scenario involves keeping atmospheric CO_2 below 400 ppm. To achieve this, people would have to drastically cut fossil fuel use worldwide over the next few decades. If the

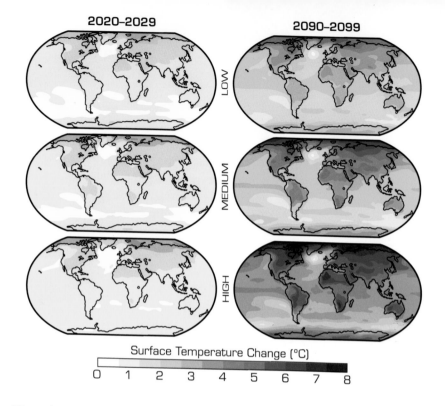

2020–2029   **2090–2099**

LOW

MEDIUM

HIGH

Surface Temperature Change (°C)

0   1   2   3   4   5   6   7   8

These images represent three different global warming futures based on climate models. The top pair shows how much temperatures will likely rise by the 2020s and by the 2090s if people drastically cut greenhouse gas emissions. The middle pair shows warming resulting from moderate emissions growth. The bottom pair shows warming from uncontrolled growth of greenhouse gas emissions.

world does this, Earth's temperature will likely rise 3.2°F (1.8°C). This number is an average. Models project the temperature could rise anywhere from 2.0°F (1.1°C) to 5.2°F (2.9°C).

The worst-case scenario reflects atmospheric CO_2 rising to about 750 ppm (more than twice its current level). This is what models predict will happen if people keep burning fossil fuels at the current rate. In this fossil fuel–intensive future, Earth's temperature could rise anywhere from 4.3°F (2.4°C) to a frightening 11.5°F (6.4°C).

CLIMATE CHANGE SKEPTICS

Global warming has been a controversial topic since it first came into the public eye in the 1980s. Initially many people, including many scientists, doubted that Earth's recent warming was anything but part of a natural climate cycle. Early climate models often gave conflicting results. Climate change skeptics used this uncertainty to support their claims that nothing out of the ordinary was happening.

But the situation has changed greatly. Scientists worldwide agree nearly unanimously that human activities are intensifying the greenhouse effect, warming the planet, and altering the climate. That doesn't mean that climate scientists agree on every detail. They continue to debate how to interpret certain kinds of data.

Unfortunately, some people use these "disagreements" to claim that many scientists doubt the reality and cause of recent global warming.

Global warming and climate change are complex topics. Understanding them requires doing what scientists are trained to do: keep an open mind, weigh the evidence carefully, and make sure you have the full story.

LIFE IN A WARMER WORLD

What do higher temperatures mean for Earth's inhabitants? Climate models paint a sobering picture of the future.

In the coming decades, global warming will likely be greatest over land and at high latitudes. Ice will keep melting. At higher latitudes, precipitation will probably increase. At lower latitudes, precipitation will tend to decrease. Hurricanes are likely to intensify. Parts of the great ocean conveyor belt could slow down. The ocean will grow ever more acidic.

Ecosystems will keep changing. If global average temperature rises more than about 4.5°F (2.5°C), 20 to 30 percent of plant and animal species will probably die out.

Global warming and climate change will affect people everywhere. More precipitation will likely improve water supplies in some places. Elsewhere, less precipitation will cause severe, prolonged droughts and water shortages. Disappearing glaciers will mean dwindling water supplies for more than one-sixth of the world's people.

Initially, more CO_2 in the air may help some plants grow faster. Crop yields are likely to increase at higher latitudes. But weeds will also grow faster. As global temperature keeps rising, crop yields will probably fall worldwide. Billions of people may face food shortages in the coming decades.

Most coastal areas will suffer from sea level rise. By 2080 millions of people will face moving to higher ground as the ocean floods coastal lands. Some small islands will be underwater.

Tens of millions of people will suffer disease, injury, and death from heat waves, floods, storms, fires, and drought. Dangerous diseases such as malaria will spread as disease-carrying insects move into new climate zones.

NO PLACE TO HIDE

Climate change will affect people on every continent and island. No one will escape its impact. The poor will suffer the most. Because they have few resources and little power, they're least able to adapt to climate change. Climate models project major changes worldwide by the mid to late twenty-first century, if not sooner.

In Africa 75 to 250 million people will probably face water shortages. In some African countries, where farmers rely on rain rather than irrigation to water their crops, yields could shrink by 50 percent. Declining harvests and drought are almost certain to bring food shortages. Rising sea level will threaten large coastal cities and low-lying river deltas. For example, the millions of people who live in Egypt's Nile River delta may have to move inland.

In Asia, glacier retreat is sure to disrupt water supplies. Normal meltwater from Himalayan glaciers feeds many rivers and lakes, providing drinking water for millions of people. As melting speeds up and glaciers disappear, so will these water supplies. Heavily populated coastal regions will face flooding from sea level rise. Higher temperatures and less rainfall are likely to reduce crop yields in parts of Asia, increasing the risk of hunger. Diseases associated with floods and droughts will probably increase across much of Asia as well.

In Australia, current water shortages are likely to worsen. Ecologically important regions such as the Great Barrier Reef could lose much of their wildlife. Coastal communities will experience more violent storms and flooding. Sea level rise will displace millions of people. As Earth warms, southern New Zealand may benefit from a longer growing season. But the risk of drought and fire will also rise.

On the whole, Europe will experience heavier precipitation and more severe floods. Parts of central and eastern Europe, however, will likely become hotter and drier. Heat waves will be worse and more common. Drought will spark more forest fires. Southern Europe will face water shortages and crop failures.

In June 2007, heavy rain and flash floods forced people from their homes in this town in northern Great Britain.

For a while, northern Europe could benefit from warmer temperatures with increased crop yields and faster-growing forests.

In South America, warmer temperatures and less rain may transform much of the Amazon rain forest into grassland. Hundreds of thousands of tropical species could go extinct. Deserts will probably expand. Extended drought may bring famine to some areas. Rising seas may submerge low-lying regions.

In North America, western mountain areas will likely see far less snow and ice. This will reduce water supplies and foster drought. Wildfires will probably increase in many places. Regions prone to heat waves will be likely to suffer more. People living along the coasts will face rising sea level and more severe storms.

For people living in the Arctic, winters will be less harsh. Ice-free waters will be easier to cross by boat. But many animals important to Arctic dwellers, such as seals, whales, and polar bears, may go extinct.

People carry signs reflecting concerns about global warming in Montreal, Canada, in 2005. This protest coincided with a United Nations climate change conference where officials were reviewing the Kyoto Protocol.

TAKING ACTION

Climate projections offer several possible futures. Which one becomes reality depends on how much—and how fast—people cut greenhouse gas emissions. To minimize climate change, people of all countries—and their governments—must change their behaviors. They must act quickly. And they must work together.

In 1992 nearly all the world's nations adopted the United Nations Framework Convention on Climate Change (UNFCCC). In 1997 UNFCCC participants adopted the Kyoto Protocol. This is an agreement intended to promote global efforts to limit greenhouse gases. It requires that developed countries who sign the agreement reduce their greenhouse gas emissions. These reductions are supposed to happen between 2008 and 2012.

Debate over the Kyoto Protocol raged for several years. Eventually, more than 170 countries signed it. All the participating countries are currently working to meet their emissions reduction targets. The United States declined to participate. The United States refused because the treaty doesn't require China, India, and several other large developing countries to reduce emissions. U.S. government officials also claimed there was too much scientific uncertainty about climate change to justify action.

The Kyoto Protocol was an important first step toward global greenhouse gas emissions reductions. It got many people to change their mind-sets and start cooperating. But even if every country in the world had signed this agreement, scientists say it wouldn't do enough. The emissions cuts aren't large enough to slow global warming.

In November 2007, UNFCCC delegates met in Bali, Indonesia, to discuss a new, stronger agreement. At the last minute, the United States agreed to participate. The Bali agreement doesn't require specific actions against global warming. It's a road map for continued negotiation—another small step in the right direction.

However, Earth needs us to take big steps. To avoid the worst-case scenario, all nations must agree to drastically cut greenhouse gas emissions. And they must do it soon.

STRATEGIES FOR A SUSTAINABLE FUTURE

How can the world reduce its greenhouse gas emissions? The most obvious answer is to reduce fossil fuel use. Fossil fuels provide almost all the energy modern societies use. So conserving energy cuts CO_2 emissions. For example, if a city uses less electricity, power plants burn less coal to generate that electricity. Hybrid and electric cars use far less energy than gas-powered cars. Riding public transportation uses less energy than driving a car.

Reusing and recycling also conserve energy. Everything people use requires energy to manufacture, process, package, or ship. Reusing something means a new item doesn't need to replace it. Recycling saves the energy needed to turn raw natural resources into finished products. It also conserves the resources themselves.

Saving energy is something everyone can do every day, starting immediately. By making a few simple lifestyle changes, people can dramatically reduce fossil fuel use and help slow global warming.

For example, compact fluorescent lightbulbs (CFLs) use about 70 percent less electricity than incandescent bulbs do. And they last about ten times longer. If every U.S. household replaced three incandescent bulbs with CFLs, U.S. CO_2 emissions would drop 23 million tons (21 million metric tons) a year. That's as much CO_2 as eleven coal-fired power plants emit per year.

CARBON-NEUTRAL LIVING

Many everyday activities consume energy and emit CO_2. Another strategy for reducing emissions is carbon-neutral living. That means eliminating as many CO_2-producing activities as possible. It can also mean offsetting (balancing) such activities with others that remove atmospheric CO_2.

A DOZEN EASY WAYS TO SAVE ENERGY

1. Turn off lights when no one's using them.
2. Turn electronics completely off. Don't leave them on standby.
3. Walk, bike, or bus instead of riding in a car.
4. If you have to travel by car, carpool with friends.
5. Look for alternatives to flying. Airplanes burn huge amounts of fuel.
6. Replace incandescent lightbulbs with CFLs (right).
7. Keep your home a few degrees cooler in winter and warmer in summer.
8. Creatively reuse and recycle everything you possibly can.
9. Take shorter showers.
10. Don't buy bottled water. Drink filtered tap water.
11. Refuse grocery store bags. Bring your own reusable bags to the store.
12. Try to eat locally grown foods rather than foods shipped long distances.

Using CFLs (top), taking the bus (center), and recycling (bottom) can save energy and reduce greenhouse gas emissions.

The first step is calculating your carbon footprint. That's a measure of the CO_2 your daily life produces. It is often expressed as tons of CO_2 or tons of carbon emitted per year. Calculating your carbon footprint takes some effort. But many websites can help you do this.

The second step is figuring out how to reduce your carbon footprint. What can you do to minimize your CO_2 emissions? Conserving energy can go a long way. So can buying locally grown food and locally made products. To help offset your CO_2 emissions, you can plant a tree or an organic garden. All the better if your planting turns a roof or a swath of pavement or bare earth into a green space. You can also buy carbon credits. For example, you might buy carbon credits from an organization that plants trees. Your money goes to planting trees that remove atmospheric CO_2. The more carbon credits people buy, the more trees get planted and the more carbon is offset.

RENEWABLE ENERGY

Replacing fossil fuels with renewable energy sources can greatly reduce greenhouse gas emissions. Renewable energy sources include hydroelectric, solar, wind, biomass, geothermal, tidal, and wave power.

Hydroelectric systems generate electricity using the power of running water. People can build small-scale hydroelectric systems along rivers or streams. They don't need a giant hydroelectric dam.

Solar power uses photovoltaic cells to convert sunlight into electricity. Every year, new types of solar cells make solar energy cheaper and more efficient.

Spinning wind turbines turn the power of moving air into

This solar tower plant near Seville, Spain, opened in March 2007. Six hundred mirrors focus sunlight on the tower, where the concentrated solar energy turns water into steam to generate electricity.

electricity. Wind turbine use has increased worldwide. Giant wind farms dot the landscape in many windy places.

Biomass is typically plant- or plant-derived material used to generate electricity or heat. Biomass might be plants grown for fuel, such as corn for ethanol or soybeans for biodiesel. It might also be plant waste or wastes left over from some other industry. Burning biomass does release CO_2. But plant biomass releases the same amount as it removed from the air while the plant was alive.

Geothermal energy is power from intense heat deep underground. This heat is plentiful in geologically active regions. People can harness it to generate electricity. They can also heat buildings directly with it.

Wave and tidal power use the cyclical movements of ocean water. People can harness this motion to generate electricity.

CARBON TRADING

Many nations have enacted laws to limit greenhouse gas emissions. These laws let factories, power plants, and other industries release a certain amount of CO_2. If a company emits more CO_2 than the law allows, it must pay a large fine. Or the company can buy carbon credits from another company that hasn't used up its emissions allowance. This exchange is called carbon trading.

Carbon trading has become an international business. The Kyoto Protocol provides a system for countries to exchange carbon credits. A nation that exceeds its CO_2 emissions allowance can buy carbon credits from another nation. The seller might be a developing country that emits very little CO_2. Or it might be an industrialized country whose emissions are below the limit.

Carbon trading is supposed to help reduce emissions. It's also intended to encourage use of cleaner energy such as solar and wind power. But critics say the system has many loopholes. If industries and nations are using these flaws to evade their climate commitments, carbon trading may not be helping much.

SHADING EARTH

Cutting emissions is the most practical way to stabilize Earth's climate. But some scientists fear that people will move too slowly. They won't cut emissions enough or in time to prevent many degrees of warming and drastic climate change.

These researchers are trying to figure out technological ways to protect the planet. A variety of strategies have emerged. The basic idea behind many of them is to deflect enough sunlight away from Earth's surface to counteract global warming.

We might, for example, be able to block sunlight within the atmosphere. One way would be to release huge amounts of sulfur dioxide gas into the upper atmosphere. Sulfur dioxide forms sulfur particles big enough to block some incoming sunlight but small enough to let heat escape back into space. However, this plan is not without risks. Adding sulfur dioxide to the air could have unpredictable side effects. This smelly toxic gas is a common pollutant in the modern world. It might worsen global warming rather than relieve it.

We might also try to shade Earth from outer space. This is a daunting technological challenge. Scientists would have to figure out how to block just the right amount of sunlight. Then engineers would have to get those sunshades into orbit. This idea might sound far-fetched. But if the future brings runaway global warming, some researchers think it might be the only way to save our planet.

TOWARD A GLOBAL SOLUTION

Global warming is a global problem. It requires a global solution. And time is running out. In late 2007, the International Energy Agency said that fossil fuel-related CO_2 emissions are set to grow from 29.8 billion tons (27 billion metric tons) in 2005 to 46.3 billion tons (42 billion metric tons) by 2030. That's a 56 percent increase. Other scientists project even faster growth.

People have the technology and creativity to slow global warming. What remains to be seen is whether we have the determination to change our ways in time.

GLOSSARY

aerosols: tiny atmospheric particles that can block solar energy and affect Earth's global average surface temperature. Air pollution and volcanic eruptions are two sources of aerosols.

algae: plantlike organisms that live mostly in water and carry out photosynthesis

atmosphere: the blanket of gases that envelops Earth

atmosphere-ocean general circulation model (AOGCM): a type of climate model that combines ocean and atmosphere circulation patterns and is used for understanding climate and predicting climate change

biomass: typically plant or plant-based material used to generate electricity or heat

carbon credit: an allowance by law to release a certain amount of carbon dioxide into the atmosphere

carbon cycle: the process by which carbon moves through Earth's atmosphere, ocean, land, and other parts of the environment

carbon dioxide (CO_2): a colorless, odorless gas made of carbon and oxygen; the greenhouse gas that contributes most to Earth's current global warming

carbon footprint: how much carbon dioxide a person, company, country, or other organization emits in a given period (usually a year)

carbon-14 dating: a method for determining the age of a living or once-living thing by measuring how much of a certain type of carbon atom it contains

carbon reservoir: a natural feature, such as a forest or landmass, that takes in carbon and stores it for a time before releasing it into the environment again

carbon trading: buying, selling, or otherwise exchanging carbon credits among the members of a group in order to stay within the group's carbon dioxide emissions limits

chlorofluorocarbons: human-made chemicals that are powerful greenhouse gases

climate: a region's average weather over a long period of time

climate change: a long-term change in the normal climate of one or more regions; the result of Earth's current global warming

climate models: complex computer programs that mathematically simulate climate and predict how climate may change as the factors affecting climate vary

climate projections: predictions about how climate may change in the future because of global warming and other factors. Scientists use climate models and vast amounts of climate data to make climate projections.

coral bleaching: algae expulsion from the bodies of reef-building corals when ocean water warms too much. Corals turn white when they lose their algae.

corals: small, stationary ocean animals that often live in colonies and most of which build stony skeletons around their soft bodies. Together, the hard outer shells of these corals form ridges called coral reefs.

deforestation: large-scale forest clearing, usually by cutting or burning

El Niño Southern Oscillation (ENSO): a pattern of wind and water changes in the tropical Pacific Ocean

foraminifera (forams): tiny creatures that drift in oceans. When forams die, their shells settle to the ocean floor and pile up in ocean sediments.

fossil fuels: carbon-rich fuels such as coal, oil, and natural gas that formed from the remains of ancient plants and animals

general circulation model (GCM): a type of climate model, primarily simulating atmospheric processes, used for weather forecasting, understanding climate, and projecting climate change

global warming: a rise in Earth's global average surface temperature

greenhouse effect: the trapping of heat radiating from Earth's sun-warmed surface by certain atmospheric gases

greenhouse gases: atmospheric gases that trap heat radiating from Earth's surface

heat sink: an environment or object that absorbs and disperses heat from another environment or object. The ocean is Earth's largest heat sink.

ice ages: periods when Earth's global average surface temperature was cool enough for large glaciers and ice sheets to cover much of the planet

ice sheets: very thick glaciers that completely bury the land and cover thousands of square miles

industrialized: characterized by the use of energy-driven machines to produce and manufacture goods

infrared radiation: invisible form of energy humans sense as heat

methane: a colorless, odorless, flammable gas produced naturally by certain bacteria in decomposition and fermentation. Atmospheric methane is a powerful greenhouse gas.

nitrous oxide: a colorless, nonflammable gas with a slightly sweet odor and taste. Atmospheric nitrous oxide is a powerful greenhouse gas.

paleoclimate: climate conditions that existed many thousands of years ago

paleoclimatologists: scientists who study Earth's ancient climate using clues from tree rings, ice sheets, lake and ocean sediments, and other natural sources

permafrost: soil, sediment, or rock that remains at or below freezing for at least two years

photosynthesis: the process by which plants, algae, and some single-celled organisms use solar energy to turn carbon dioxide and water into sugar and oxygen

photovoltaic: generating an electric current when exposed to sunlight

plankton: a vast population of tiny organisms that drift in the upper layers of the ocean and large lakes. Plankton is the base of nearly all aquatic food chains.

pollen: dustlike grains produced by flowering plants. Pollen grains contain reproductive cells that help plants make seeds.

radioactive: releasing potentially harmful energy during gradual atomic breakdown

radiosonde: a balloon with instruments that measure temperature, humidity, and air pressure at different altitudes and send the data via radio signals to receivers on the ground

renewable energy sources: energy sources that cannot be used up, such as sunlight and wind

salinity: saltiness

satellite: an object orbiting a planet to gather and transmit scientific data

sea ice: ice that forms on the ocean when surface waters freeze

sea level: a measure of ocean water volume. Sea level measurements show how high onto land the ocean reaches.

sediments: particles suspended in water that eventually sink to form a solid layer of mud on the bottom of an ocean, lake, or river

sunspots: cooler patches that form on the sun's surface. Sunspots appear darker than the area surrounding them.

sustainable: able to be maintained without destroying the environment

thermal expansion: the tendency of substances to expand as they warm

thermohaline circulation: the pattern of deep ocean currents that carry heat around Earth; also called the great ocean conveyor belt

tree rings: layers of new wood produced annually just under the bark of a tree's trunk. The layers appear as rings in a trunk cut crosswise.

tundra: a cold, treeless environment found in the Arctic and on the top of mountains

ultraviolet radiation: a form of solar energy invisible to human eyes. It is more powerful than visible light and can cause sunburn.

visible light: solar energy that humans can see

water vapor: an invisible, gaseous form of water

SOURCE NOTES

9 Public Broadcasting Service, "Bruce Molnia: U.S. Geological Survey," *Journey to Planet Earth: Interviews with Experts*, 2007, http://www.pbs.org/journeytoplanetearth/about/expert_pdfs/molnia.pdf (February 14, 2008).

11 David W. Schindler, "The Mysterious Missing Sink," *Nature*, March 1999, 105–106.

22 Roger Revelle and Hans E. Suess, "Carbon Dioxide Exchange between Atmosphere and Ocean and the Question of an Increase of Atmospheric CO_2 during the Past Decades," *Tellus*, September 1957, 18–27.

25 NOAA Paleoclimatology Program, "A Paleo Perspective on Global Warming," *World Data Center for Paleoclimatology*, August 31, 2007, http://www.ncdc.noaa.gov/paleo/globalwarming/home.html (February 18, 2008).

41 Intergovernmental Panel on Climate Change, "IPCC Second Assessment Synthesis of Scientific-Technical Information Relevant to Interpreting Article 2 of the UN Framework Convention on Climate Change," *IPCC Reports*, 1995, http://www.ipcc.ch/pdf/climate-changes-1995/2nd-assessment-synthesis.pdf (January 12, 2008).

45 Catherine Brahic, "Blame for Global Warming Placed Firmly on Humankind," *New Scientist Environment*, February 5, 2007, http://environment.newscientist.com/channel/earth/dn11088-blame-for-global-warming-placed-firmly-on-humankind.html (February 10, 2007).

51 Tom Clynes, "Konrad Steffen: The Global Warming Prophet," *Popular Science*, July 3, 2007, http://www.popsci.com/popsci/science/6661e3568cc83110vgnvcm1000004eecbccdrcrd.html (October 3, 2007).

56 Earle Holland, "Ice Caps in Africa, Tropical South America Likely to Disappear within 15 Years," *Ohio State University Research News*, February 18, 2001, http://researchnews.osu.edu/archive/glacgone.htm (February 10, 2008).

61 Bruce Lieberman, "Ocean Warming, Fossil Fuel Gases Linked," *SignOnSanDiego*, February 18, 2005, http://www.signonsandiego.com/news/science/20050218-9999-7m18ocean.html (November 2, 2007).

65   Rob Gutro, "NASA Study Finds World Warmth Edging Ancient Levels," *NASA Goddard Space Flight Center News*, September 25, 2006, http://www.nasa.gov/centers/goddard/news/topstory/2006/world_warmth.html (September 1, 2007).

72   University Corporation for Atmospheric Research, "Expect a Warmer, Wetter World This Century, Computer Models Agree," *NCAR and UCAR News Center*, October 19, 2006, http://www.ucar.edu/news/releases/2006/wetterworld.shtml (August 12, 2007).

73   Michael Reilly, "Dry Future Ahead for the U.S. Southwest," *New Scientist Environment*, April 14, 2007, http://environment.newscientist.com/channel/earth/mg19425994.600-dry-future-ahead-for-the-us-southwest.html (July 21, 2007).

82   Les Blumenthal, "Oceans' Growing Acidity Worries Scientists," *McClatchy Newspapers*, December 16, 2007, http://www.mcclatchydc.com/244/story/23138.html (December 16, 2007).

83   Lee Clippard, "Global Warming Increases Species Extinctions Worldwide, University of Texas at Austin Researcher Finds," *The University of Texas at Austin: News*, November 14, 2006, http://www.utexas.edu/news/2006/11/14/biology (June 12, 2007).

83   University of Leeds, "Climate Change Threatens a Million Species with Extinction," *University of Leeds: Media*, January 7, 2004, http://www.leeds.ac.uk/media/current/extinction.htm, (November 22, 2007).

85   Pat Joseph, "Start by Arming Yourself with Knowledge: Al Gore Breaks Through with His Global-Warming Message," *Sierra*, September–October 2006, 59.

85   Richard Black, "UN Challenges States on Warming," *BBC News*, November 17, 2007, http://news.bbc.co.uk/2/hi/science/nature/7098902.stm (November 17, 2007).

SELECTED BIBLIOGRAPHY

Anderson, Alun. "100 Days on Thin Ice." *New Scientist*, November 17, 2007, 54–55.

Appenzeller, Tim. "The Big Thaw." *National Geographic Magazine*, June 2007, 56–71.

Black, Richard. "Earth—Melting in the Heat?" *BBC News*. May 18, 2007. http://news.bbc.co.uk/2/hi/science/nature/4315968.stm (May 18, 2007).

Blackwell Publishing. "North American Birds Moving North as a Result of Climate Change." *ScienceDaily*. June 14, 2007. http://www.sciencedaily.com/releases/2007/06/070611112536.htm (November 9, 2007).

Brahic, Catherine. "Blame for Global Warming Placed Firmly on Humankind." *New Scientist Environment*. February 5, 2007. http://environment.newscientist.com/channel/earth/dn11088-blame-for-global-warming-placed-firmly-on-humankind.html (February 13, 2007).

Brahic, Catherine, David L. Chandler, Michael Le Page, Phil McKenna, and Fred Pearce. "Climate Myths." *New Scientist*, May 19, 2007, 34–42.

British Broadcasting Corporation. "Climate Scepticism: The Top 10." *BBC News*. November 12, 2007. http://news.bbc.co.uk/2/hi/in_depth/629/629/7074601.stm (December 11, 2007).

———. "Planet under Pressure: In Depth." *BBC News*. August 15, 2007. http://news.bbc.co.uk/2/hi/in_depth/sci_tech/2004/planet/default.stm (September 6, 2007).

Cook, A. J., A. J. Fox, D. G. Vaughan, and J. G. Ferrigno. "Retreating Glacier Fronts on the Antarctic Peninsula over the Past Half-Century." *Science*, April 22, 2005, 541–544.

Dessler, Andrew E., and Edward A. Parson. *The Science and Politics of Global Climate Change*. New York: Cambridge University Press, 2006.

Dow, Kirstin, and Thomas E. Downing. *The Atlas of Climate Change: Mapping the World's Greatest Challenge*. Berkeley: University of California Press, 2007.

Emanuel, Kerry. "Increasing Destructiveness of Tropical Cyclones over the Past 30 Years." *Nature*, August 4, 2005, 686–688.

Gore, Al. *An Inconvenient Truth: The Planetary Emergency of Global Warming and What We Can Do about It*. Emmaus, PA: Rodale, 2006.

Hansen, James. "Climate Catastrophe." *New Scientist*, July 28, 2007, 30–33.

Intergovernmental Panel on Climate Change. "Fourth Assessment Report: Climate Change 2007." *IPCC Reports.* 2007. http://www.ipcc.ch/ipccreports/assessments-reports.htm (February 18, 2008).

Met Office Hadley Centre. "Climate Change and the Greenhouse Effect: A Briefing from the Hadley Centre." *Met Office Hadley Centre Brochures.* December 2005. http://www.metoffice.gov.uk/research/hadleycentre/pubs/brochures/2005/climate_greenhouse.pdf (February 18, 2008).

National Geographic Society. "Effects of Global Warming." *National Geographic: Environment.* 2007. http://green.nationalgeographic.com/environment/global-warming/gw-effects.html (October 2, 2007).

Nature Conservancy. "Climate Change Impacts." *The Nature Conservancy: Initiatives.* N.d. http://www.nature.org/initiatives/climatechange/strategies/art21202.html (May 19, 2007).

NOAA Paleoclimatology Program. "A Paleo Perspective on Global Warming." *World Data Center for Paleoclimatology.* November 10, 2006. http://www.ncdc.noaa.gov/paleo/globalwarming/index.html (October 11, 2007).

Pearce, Fred. *With Speed and Violence: Why Scientists Fear Tipping Points in Climate Change.* Boston: Beacon Press, 2007.

Pew Center on Global Climate Change. "Climate Change 101: International Action." *Pew Center on Global Climate Change: Global Warming Basics.* 2006. http://www.pewclimate.org/docUploads/PEW_Climate%20101%20Intl.pdf (July 7, 2007).

Riebeek, Holli. "Global Warming." *NASA Earth Observatory.* May 11, 2007. http://earthobservatory.nasa.gov/Library/GlobalWarmingUpdate/global_warming_update.html (November 16, 2007).

Sakai, Jill. "Global Warming Forecasts Creation, Loss of Climate Zones." *University of Wisconsin–Madison News.* March 26, 2007. http://www.news.wisc.edu/13600 (December 12, 2007).

Scripps Institution of Oceanography. "Scripps CO2 Program." *Scripps Institution of Oceanography.* 2008. http://scrippsco2.ucsd.edu/home/index.php (January 7, 2008).

TerraNature Trust. "Melting Permafrost Methane Emissions: The Other Threat to Climate Change." *TerraNature.* September 15, 2006. http://www.terranature.org/methaneSiberia.htm (December 5, 2007).

Weart, Spencer. *The Discovery of Global Warming.* Cambridge, MA: Harvard University Press, 2003.

———. "The Discovery of Global Warming." *Center for History of Physics: Online Exhibits.* August 2007. http://www.aip.org/history/climate (August 18, 2007).

FURTHER READING AND WEBSITES

BOOKS

David, Laurie, and Cambria Gordon. *The Down-to-Earth Guide to Global Warming*. New York: Orchard Books, 2007.

Gershon, David. *Low Carbon Diet: A 30 Day Program to Lose 5000 Pounds*. Woodstock, NY: Empowerment Institute, 2006.

Thornhill, Jan. *This Is My Planet: The Kids Guide to Global Warming*. Toronto: Maple Tree Press, 2007.

Time. *Global Warming*. Minneapolis: Twenty-First Century Books, 2008.

WEBSITES

BBC Climate Change
http://news.bbc.co.uk/2/hi/science/nature/portal/climate_change/default.stm

This site is a good source for clear explanations of many aspects of the greenhouse effect, global warming, and climate change. It also provides up-to-date reports on climate change research and discoveries.

Climate Choices
http://www.climatechoices.org/ne

This interactive website created by the Union of Concerned Scientists helps users visualize the impacts of climate change in two key regions of the United States, as well as learn more about actions residents are taking to cut carbon emissions and cope with global warming.

Climate Connections: A Global Journey
http://www.npr.org/news/specials/climate/interactive/?ps=bb4

This interactive website created by National Public Radio lets readers see and hear about the impacts of climate change on people in many different parts of the world.

Climate Timeline
http://www.ngdc.noaa.gov/paleo/ctl/overview.html

This interactive timeline developed jointly by the National Oceanic and Atmospheric Administration's National Geophysical Data Center and Paleoclimatology Program allows users to explore climatic information at varying scales through time.

Earth Observatory: Experiments and Features
http://earthobservatory.nasa.gov/Laboratory/PlanetEarthScience/
GlobalWarming/GW.html
http://earthobservatory.nasa.gov/Library/GlobalWarmingUpdate/global_
warming_update.html
> These two NASA websites give clear but in-depth overviews of the greenhouse effect and global warming. They also offer features about how scientists are currently studying climate change and its impacts on Earth's environments and inhabitants using satellites and other tools.

Intergovernmental Panel on Climate Change (IPCC)
http://www.ipcc.ch
> This is the IPCC's official website. It provides links to all four IPCC assessments on global warming and climate change, as well as many other articles and reports.

Larsen Ice Shelf
http://na.unep.net/digital_atlas2/webatlas.php?id=265
> This UN Environment Programme website shows illustrations of Antarctica's major ice shelves and satellite images of the Larsen Ice Shelf breakup.

National Geographic Climate Connections
http://ngm.nationalgeographic.com/ngm/climateconnections
> Users can read articles and view pictures on climate change and its impacts worldwide at this website created by *National Geographic* magazine.

National Snow and Ice Data Center
http://nsidc.org
> At this site, users can learn about U.S. and international scientific investigations of snow, ice, and global warming worldwide.

Pew Center on Global Climate Change
http://www.pewclimate.org
> This website is a sound source for current news and scientific reports on global warming and climate change.

ScienceDaily Earth and Climate News
http://www.sciencedaily.com/news/earth_climate
> This site is a comprehensive and current source for the latest scientific research about many aspects of climate change and its impacts.

World Wildlife Fund
http://www.panda.org/about_wwf/what_we_do/climate_change/what_
you_can_do/index.cfm
> Readers who visit this section of the World Wildlife Fund's website can learn ways to help slow global warming and climate change. It includes an "Ecological Footprint Quiz" and a link to a carbon footprint calculator.

INDEX

aerosols, 27, 33–34
Africa, 90
air pollution, 27
Alaskan glaciers, 7, 54–55
Alps, European, 55
Amazon rain forest, 80–81
Andes mountain glaciers, 55–56
animals: life cycle changes, 77–78; range shifts, 78–79; species extinctions, 82–83
Antarctica: glaciers, 12; ice cores, 32; ice melt in, 52–54
Arctic: climate change, 91; ice shelves, 48; sea ice melting, 46–50
Argo program, 60–61
Arrhenius, Svante August, 19
Asia, 90
atmosphere. *See* greenhouse effect
atmosphere-ocean general circulation climate models, 39
atmospheric CO_2: and Amazon rain forest, 81; and global surface temperatures, 33; increases in, 41; measuring, 18–19, 20, 22–23; from thawing tundra, 66–67
Australia, 74, 90; glaciers, 12

Bali agreement, 93
Barnett, Tim, 61
Bering Sea, 78–79
biomass power, 97
British Antarctica Survey (BAS), 52–53
Byrd Polar Research Center (BPRC), 55

Callendar, Guy Stewart, 19–20
carbon cycle, 16–19, 20–22
carbon dioxide (CO_2), 15–16, *See also* atmospheric CO_2
carbon-14 dating, 20–22
carbon-neutral living, 94–96
carbon trading, 98
Chamberlain, T. C., 19
chlorofluorocarbons (CFCs), 38, 41
climate changes: historical, 12–13; observed, 8. *See also* ecosystem changes
climate models, 35–39, 40, 54, 61
coal power, 18
compact fluorescent light-bulbs (CFLs), 94
computers, climate models and, 35–39
Cook, Alison, 52
Cooperative Institute for Research in Environmental Sciences (CIRES), 51
corals, 79–80

Dansercoer, Dixie, 48
droughts, 70, 72–75, 81

ecosystem changes, 79–82; Arctic tundra, 66–68; climate zone movement, 69–70; season changes, 77–78; weather extremes, 70–77
El Niño Southern Oscillation (ENSO), 34, 77
energy conservation methods, 94–97
equatorial zone, 70, 79–82
Europe, climate change in, 71, 72, 90–91
Feely, Richard, 82
floods, 72–73
foraminifera (forams), 30
fossil fuels, 17, 20
Fourier, Jean-Baptiste Joseph, 13, 17

general circulation climate models, 36–38
geothermal power, 97
Glacier Bay National Park, 7
glaciers: glaciation process, 11–13; mountain, 54–56; retreat and melting, 7–8, 52
global warming, 8–9; concern for, 9; controversy and skepticism, 40–41, 88; future scenarios, 86–88; protests and politics, 92–93; scientists speak out, 39–40, 85
Gravity Recovery and Climate Experiment (GRACE), 58
Great Barrier Reef, 80, 90
greenhouse effect, 13, 14–15; discovered, 17; fossil carbon effects, 20–22; greenhouse gases, 38; reducing emissions, 92–98
Greenland ice sheet, 32, 44–45, 51–52

Hadley Centre for Climate Prediction and Research, 37, 73
Hansen, James E., 39–40
heat waves, 70–71
Himalayan mountain glaciers, 55

Hogbom, Arvid Gustaf, 17–19
Hubert, Alain, 48
hurricanes, 75–77, 89
hydroelectric power, 96

ice core data, 31–33
Intergovernmental Panel on Climate Change (IPCC) reports, 41–43, 85
International Geophysical Year, 26

Keeling, Charles David, 22–23, 25
Keeling curve, 23
Kirpotin, Sergei, 68
Kyoto Protocol, 93

La Niña, 34
Larsen Ice Shelf, 53
Lawrence Livermore National Laboratory, 61

Maslowski, Wieslaw, 48
Mauna Loa, 22
McKenney, Daniel, 69
methane, 38, 41, 67–68
Molnia, Bruce, 7, 54
Muir Glacier, 6–7

National Center for Atmospheric Research (NCAR), 72, 77
New Zealand, 55; glaciers, 12
nitrous oxide, 38, 41
North America: climate change in, 91; glaciers, 12; tree species' climates, 69–70

oceans: climate change, 81–82; CO_2 absorption, 19, 21; ocean currents, 34, 62–63; sea level rise, 56–59; sediments and

paleoclimate, 30–31; temperature rise, 59–61

paleoclimate, Earth's, 28–33, 40
Parmesan, Camille, 82–83
permafrost, 66
photosynthesis, 16, 19
Pierce, David, 61
plants: life cycle changes, 77–78; species extinctions, 82–83
polar bears, 50
pollen and paleoclimate, 29–30
precipitation, global changes, 72–75

radiosonde, 26
rainfall changes, 72–75
rain forests, 80–81
Ramanathan, Veerabhadran, 38
renewable energy, 96–97
Revelle, Roger, 21–22

satellites: GRACE program, 58; sea ice measurement, 47; sea level measurement, 57; temperature measurement using, 26
Scambos, Ted, 53
Scripps Institution of Oceanography, 21, 61
sea ice, 8, 46–50
sea level rise, 56–59
seasons, changes in, 77–78
sediment cores, 30–31
Siberian tundra, 68
solar energy, 14, 35
solar power, 96, 97
South America, 12, 91
Steffen, Konrad, 51
storms, severe, 75–77
Suess, Hans, 20–22
surface temperature, global: and CO_2 correlation, 33;

since 1860, 9; historical data gathering, 25–27

Tasman Glacier, 55
Tebaldi, Claudia, 72
thermohaline circulation, 62–63
Thomas, Chris, 83
Thompson, Lonnie, 55–56
tidal power, 97
Ting, Ming Fang, 73
TOPEX/Poseidon satellite, 57
Tottenham Glacier, 54
trees: effects on, 69–70; and paleoclimate, 28–29
Trenberth, Kevin, 77
Tropical Rainfall Measuring Mission (TRMM), 73
tropics, climate change in, 70, 79–82
tundra, Arctic, 66–68
Tyndall, John, 15, 17

United Kingdom, 71, 72
United Nations Environment Programme (UNEP), 41
United Nations Framework Convention on Climate Change (UNFCCC), 93
Urey, Harold, 30
U.S. Geological Survey, 7

volcanic activity, 27, 33–34

Wadhams, Peter, 48
Ward Hunt Ice Shelf, 48–49
weather extremes: floods and droughts, 72–75; heat waves, 70–72; severe storms, 75–77
weather models, 35–36
Webster, Peter, 77
wildfires, 74–75
wind power, 96–97
World Meteorological Organization (WMO), 40–41

ABOUT THE AUTHOR

Rebecca L. Johnson is the award-winning author of dozens of books for young adults. She has written on topics ranging from Antarctica to the deep sea. Critics have recognized many of her books as outstanding examples of science writing.

Global warming and climate change have interested Johnson for a long time, and she has interacted with climate scientists from many different countries. Nearly twenty years ago, she published her first book on global warming, *The Greenhouse Effect: Life on a Warmer Planet,* which won the 1990 Science Book Award from the Society of School Librarians International. While Johnson wrote *Investigating Climate Change,* she was struck by the number of climate projections that have come true since her first book on this subject. Johnson lives in Sioux Falls, South Dakota, where winters have become noticeably warmer over the past two decades.

PHOTO ACKNOWLEDGMENTS

The images in this book are used with the permission of: © Ira Block/National Geographic/Getty Images, backgrounds; © Momatiuk - Eastcott/CORBIS, p. 1; NASA, pp. 2, 47 (both), 76; Molina, Bruce F. 2004. *Muir Glacier:* From the *Glacier photograph collection.* National Snow and Ice Data Center/World Data Center for Glaciology. Courtesy of the U.S. Geological Survey, p. 6; Field, William O. 1941. *Muir Glacier:* From the *Glacier photograph collection.* National Snow and Ice Data Center/World Data Center for Glaciology, p. 6 (inset); © 2008 Climatic Research Unit, p. 9; © Dr. Marli Miller/Visuals Unlimited, p. 10; © Laura Westlund/Independent Picture Service (IPS), pp. 12, 15, 57, 62; Ron Miller, p. 17; © age fotostock/SuperStock, p. 18; Scripps Institution of Oceanography/UC San Diego, p. 23; © British Antarctic Survey/Photo Researchers, Inc., p. 24; © Photodisc/Getty Images, pp. 28, 50; © Gary Braasch, pp. 31, 68; © Vin Morgan/AFP/Getty Images, p. 32; Chart by Laura Westlund/IPS. Based on data from Petit, J.R., et al., 2001, Vostok Ice Core Data for 420,000 Years, IGBP PAGES/World Data Center for Paleoclimatology Data Contribution Series #2001-076. NOAA/NGDC Paleoclimatology Program, p. 33; Climate models © British Crown Copyright 2005, the Met Office. Illustrated by Laura Westlund/IPS, p. 37; © British Crown Copyright 2005, the Met Office, p. 42 (both); © Roger Braithwaite/Peter Arnold, Inc., p. 44; © NHPA/Bryan & Cherry Alexander, p. 49; Japan Coast Guard/Argo Information Centre, http://argo.jcommops.org, p. 60; © Pete Oxford/Minden Pictures/Getty Images, p. 64; © Arif Ali/AFP/Getty Images, p. 71; © Ian Waldie/Getty Images, p. 74; © Brandon Cole/Visuals Unlimited, p. 79; AP Photo/Pervez Masih, p. 84; Data © 2007 IPCC WG1-AR4. Illustrated by Laura Westlund/IPS, p. 87; AP Photo/Dave Thompson, p. 91; AP Photo/Ian Barrett, CP, p. 92; © Todd Strand/Independent Picture Service, p. 95 (all); © Denis Doyle/Getty Images, p. 97.

Cover: © Momatiuk - Eastcott/CORBIS.

Photo: SYLVIE JACQUEMIN/DAVID TATE

IN 1990 I RELEASED A SOLO PIANO ALBUM CALLED "PIANISSIMO." MOST OF THE SONGS IN THIS BOOK ARE ON THAT ALBUM. THE PLAYING TECHNIQUE OF MY MUSIC IS NOT OVERLY DEMANDING, I THINK - BUT THE EMOTIONAL INTENT IS VERY IMPORTANT. I AM HAPPY THAT THE MUSIC WILL BE GIVEN NEW LIFE THROUGH YOUR FINGERS.

Suzanne Ciani

Photo: MICHAEL MILLER

Photos on pages 1, 14, 46, 56, 76 and 90 by Sylvie Jacquemin/David Tate unless otherwise identified

ADAGIO

A dream is lost, broken — who knows why?

By SUZANNE CIANI

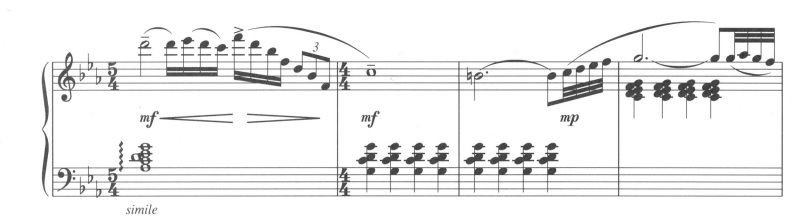

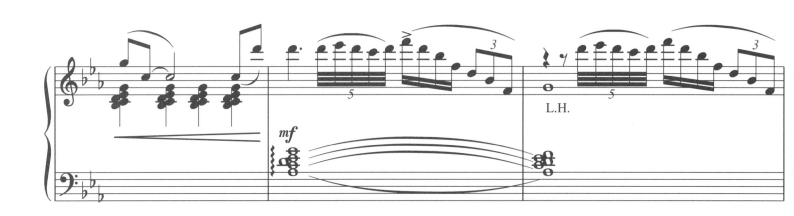

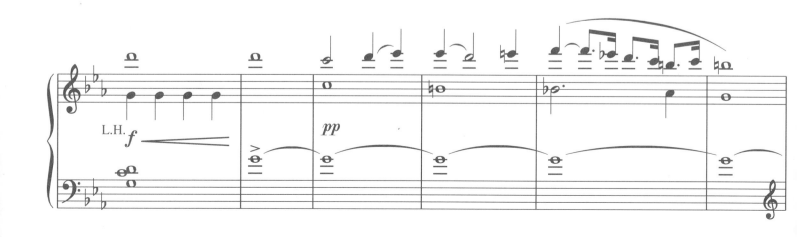

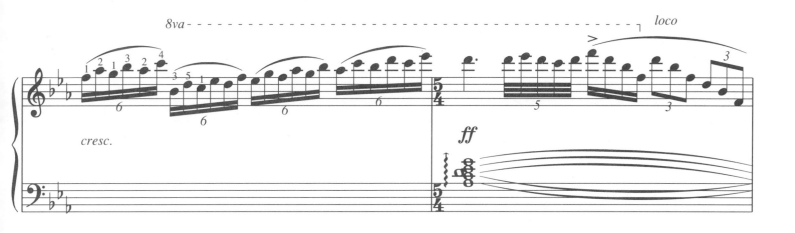

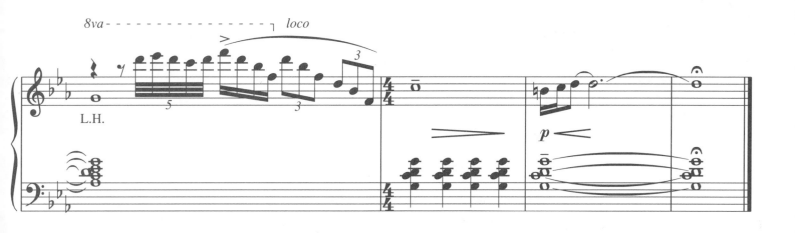

AEGEAN WAVE

I've never actually sailed on the Aegean Ocean, but this is how it would be.

By SUZANNE CIANI

For shorter piece, go to Coda ⊕ here

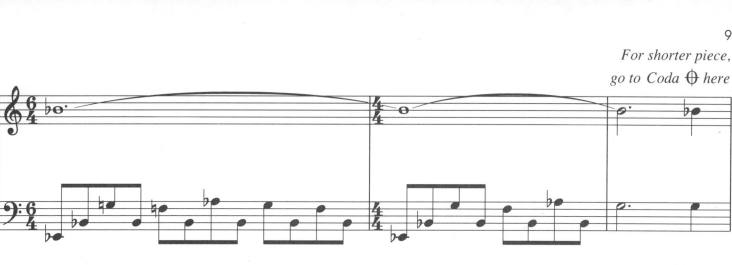

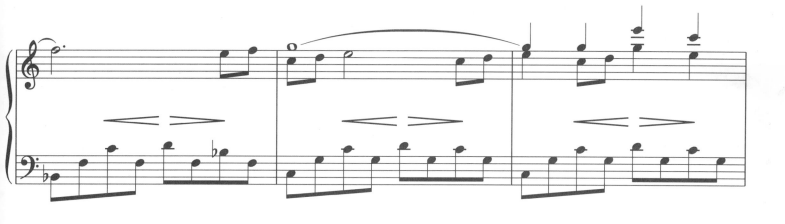

8va - - - ⌐

8va - - - - - - - - - - - -

D.S. al Coda

⊕ *Coda*

improvise fill w. R.H.
if desired

mp

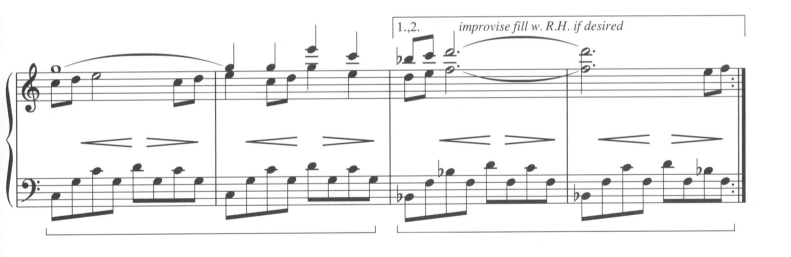

1.,2.   *improvise fill w. R.H. if desired*

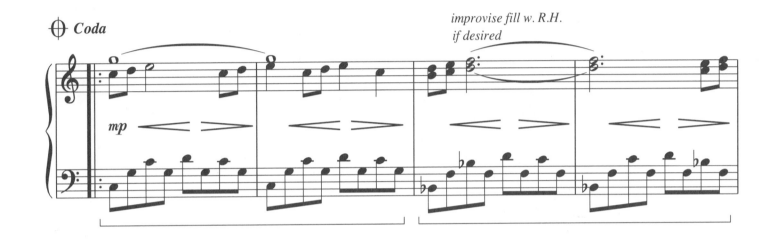

3.

ANTHEM

I have dedicated ANTHEM to the Chinese students in
Tiannenman Square on June 4, 1989 — in celebration of their
spirit and commitment

By SUZANNE CIANI

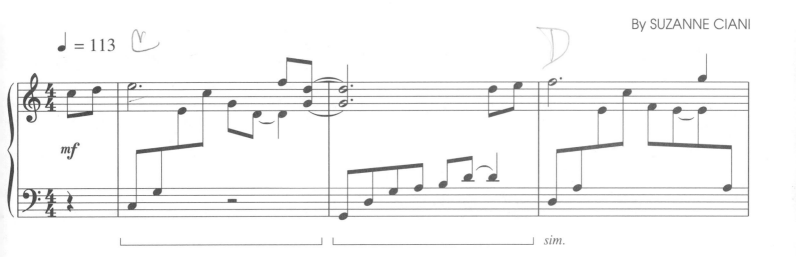

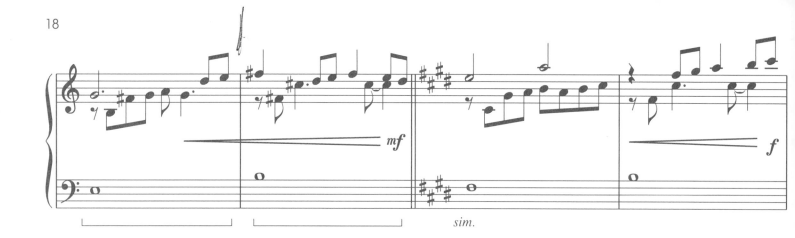

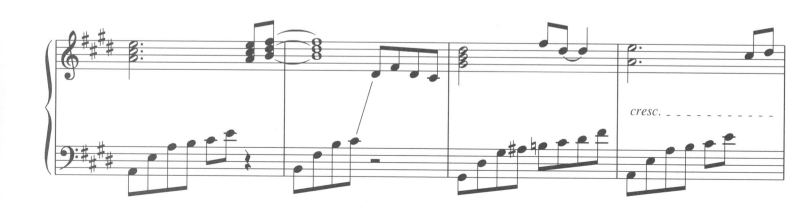

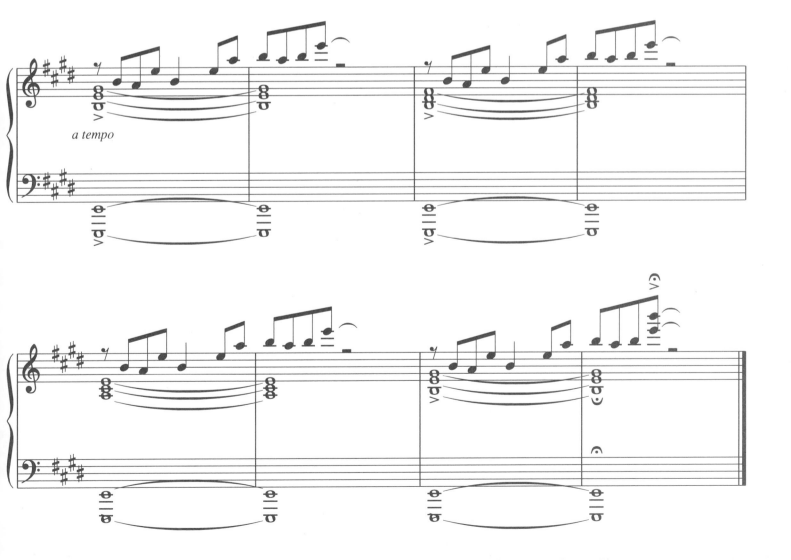

DRIFTING

Drifting is the movie of the clouds. Shapes and images come and go.

By SUZANNE CIANI

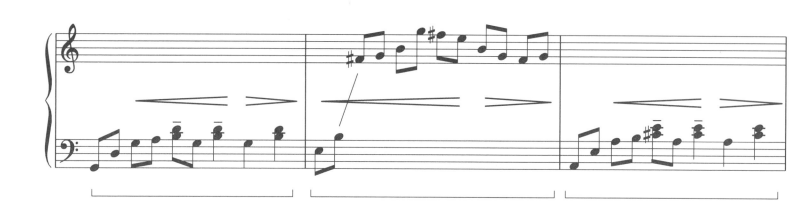

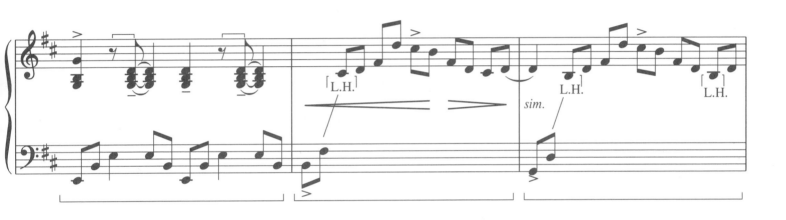

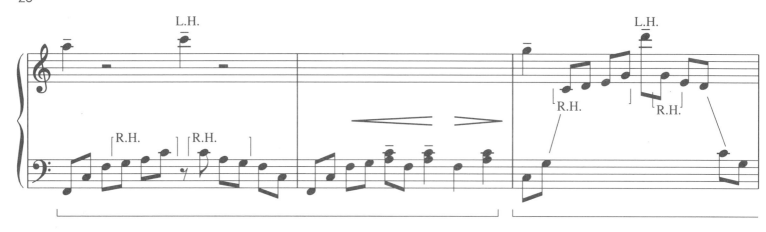

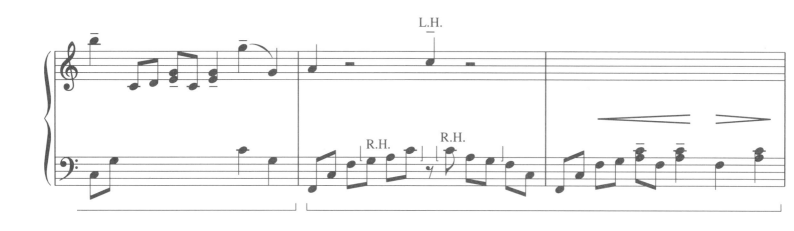

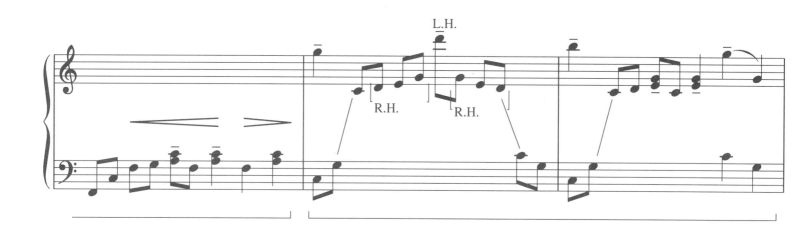

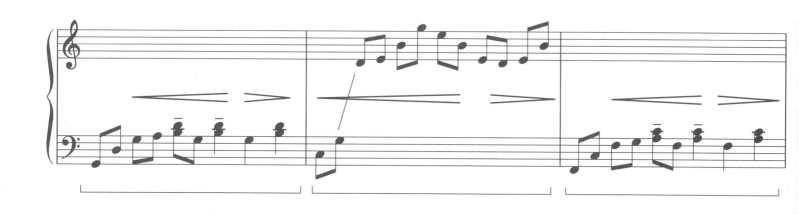

EAGLE

This song was co-written with a friend and is about running and feeling free.

By SUZANNE CIANI
and TAMARA KLINE

2nd time to %

C

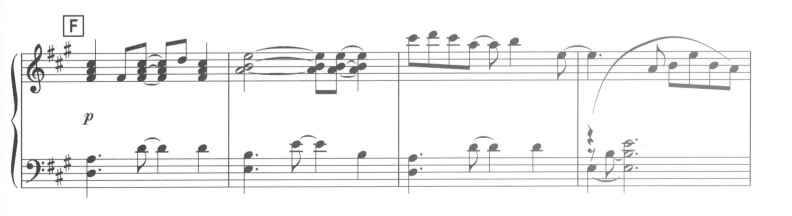

THE FIFTH WAVE: LULLABY of the SEA

My earlier compositions were all called "waves" - partly because they built, climaxed and receded, as this piece does.

By SUZANNE CIANI

Right hand can be freely improvised on harmonies indicated.

E/B   F♯/B

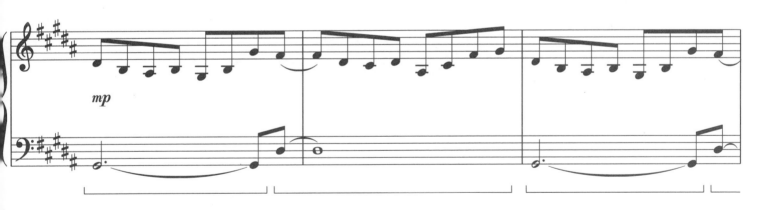

B

mp

cresc.

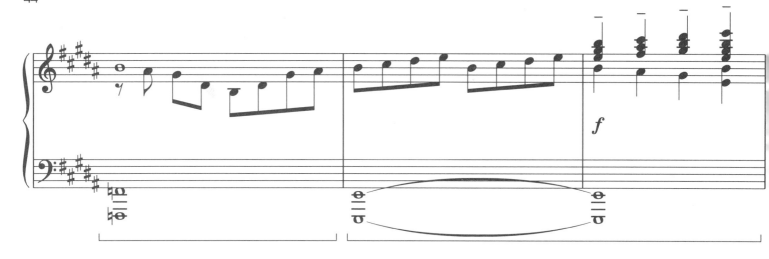

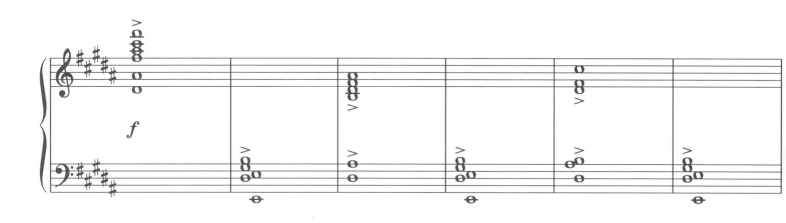

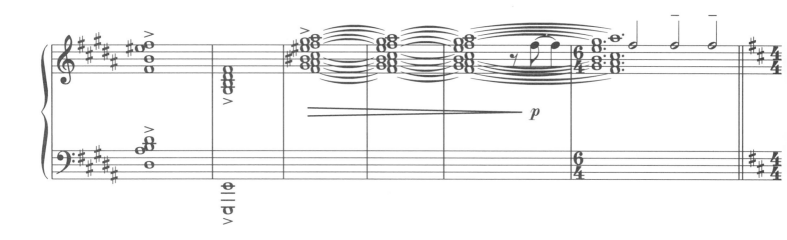

Repeat Ad Lib. and Fade

INVERNESS

This piece is based on Respighi's "Notturno" which I played
as a child. It was also inspired by the natural beauty of
Inverness, California.

By SUZANNE CIANI

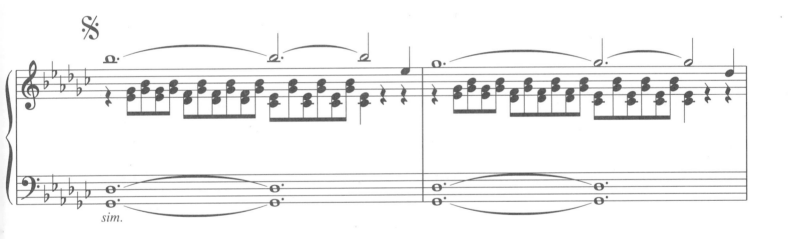

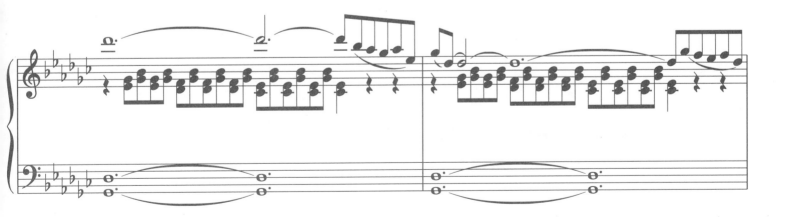

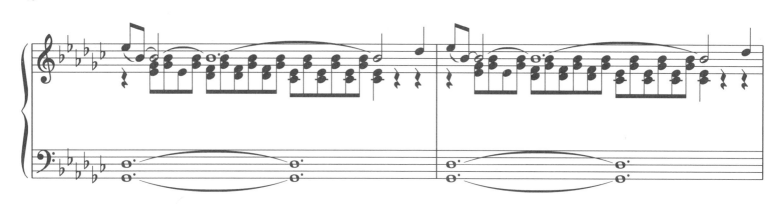

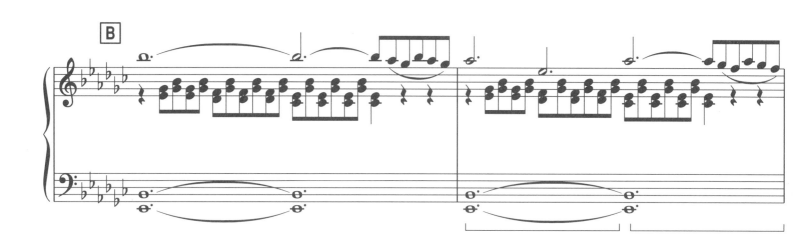

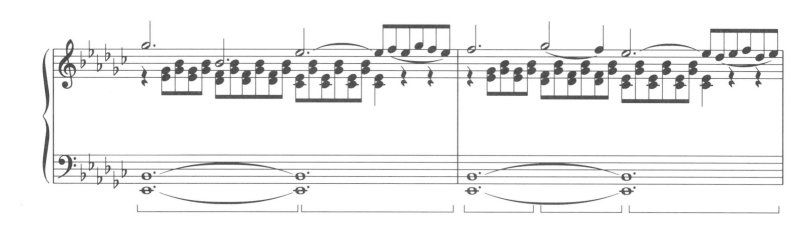

To Coda ⊕

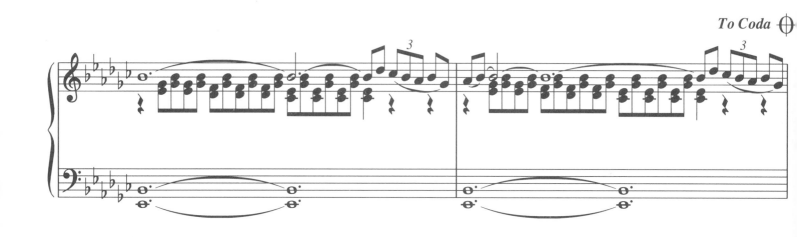

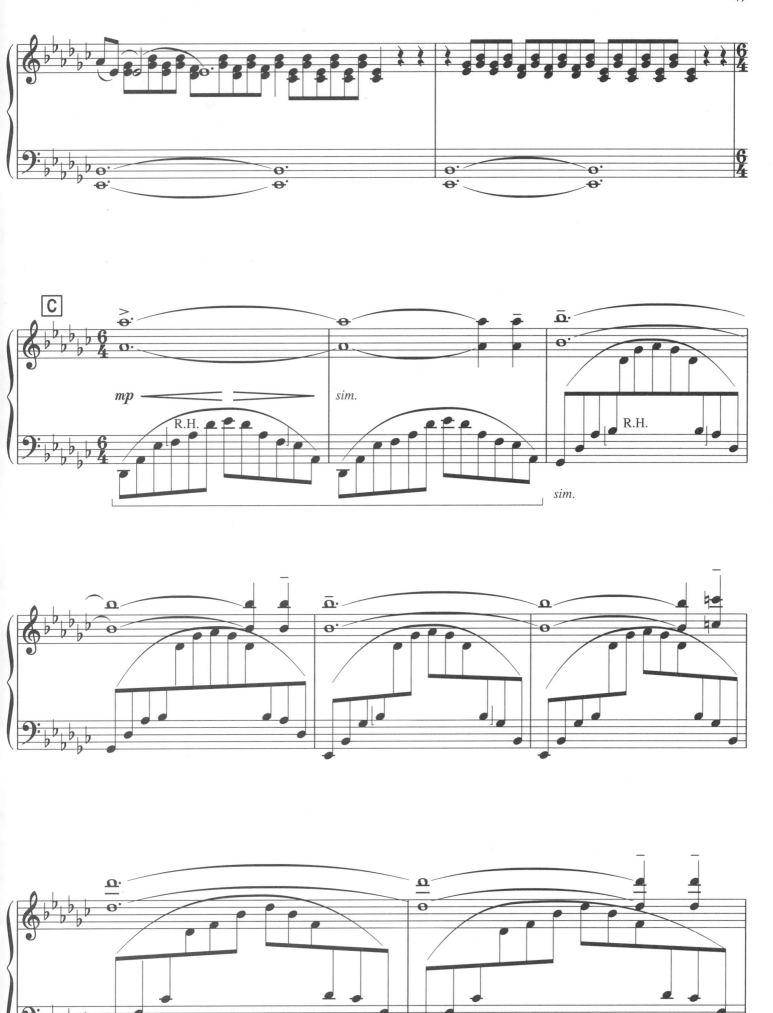

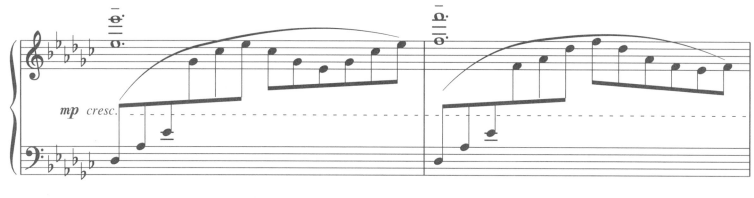

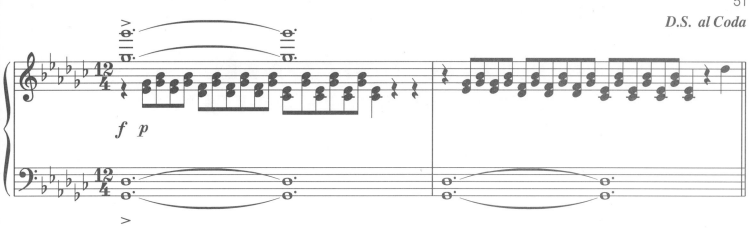

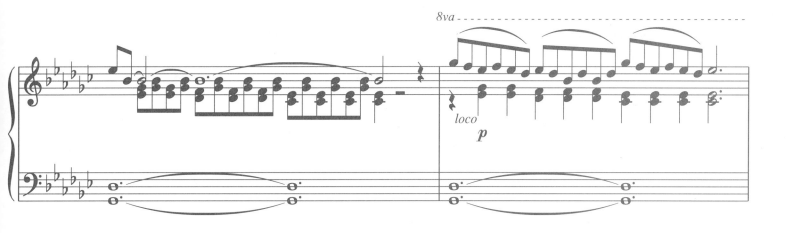

LIFE IN THE MOONLIGHT

Ritual dancing on a desert oasis, under the full moon light...

By SUZANNE CIANI

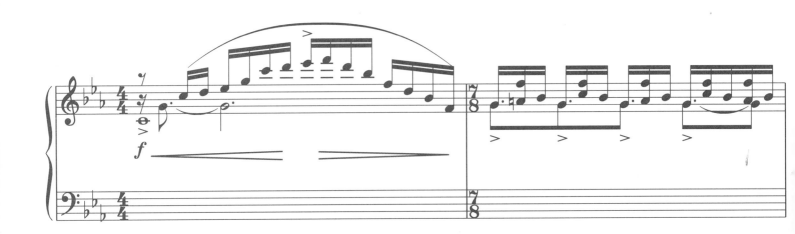

MOTHER'S SONG

*Written for the film about Mother Teresa, the melody seems to
say her name.*

By SUZANNE CIANI

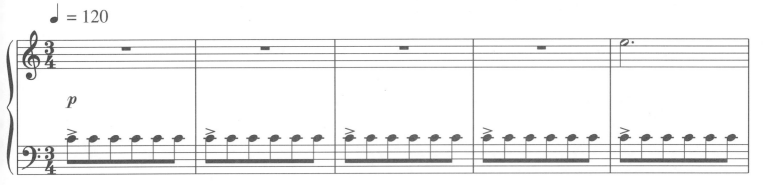

pedal down until *

8va bassa

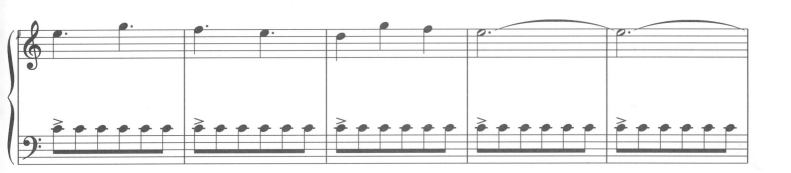

R.H.

8va bassa

(L.H.)

mp

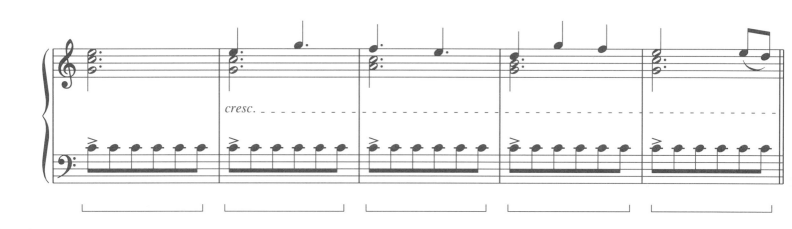

cresc.

mf

sim.

cresc.

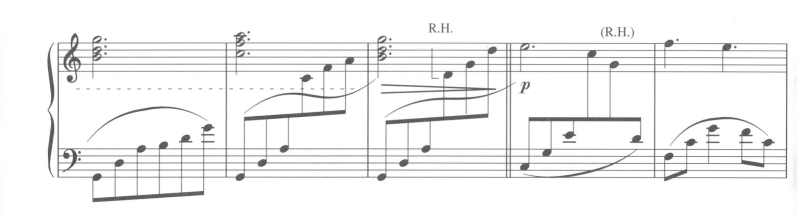

R.H.

(R.H.)

p

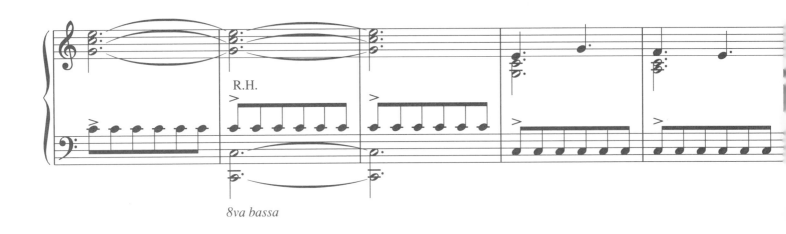

MOZART

Inspired by one of my favorite composers, this piece is not exactly the way he would have done it.

By SUZANNE CIANI

sim.

62

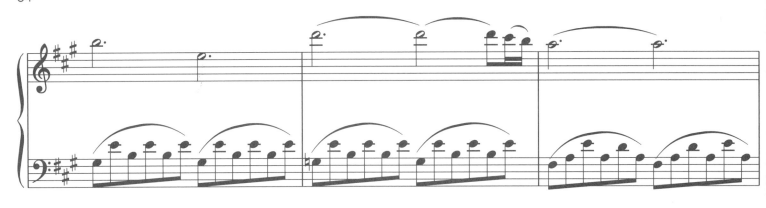

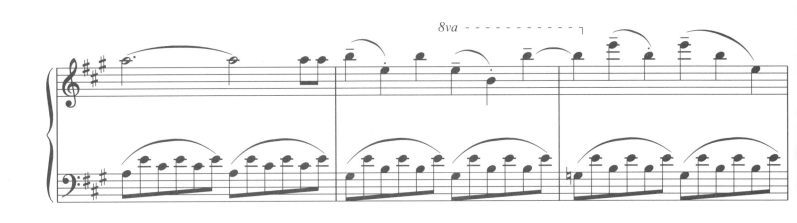

NEVERLAND

A gallop through the forest on the perfect horse—
and a mystery encounter

By SUZANNE CIAN

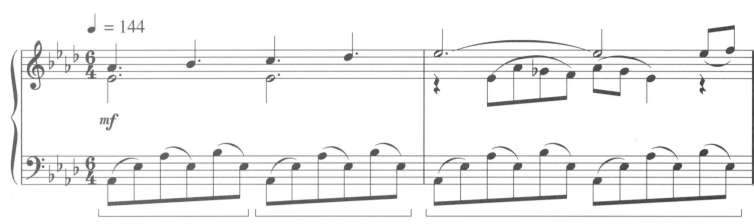

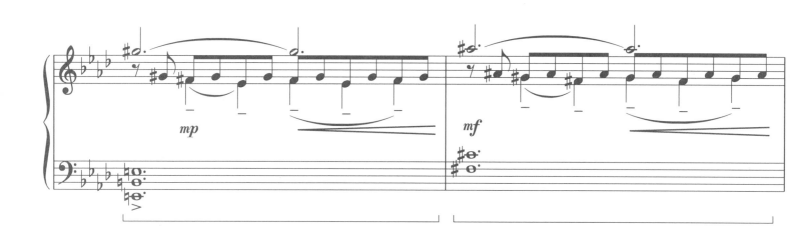

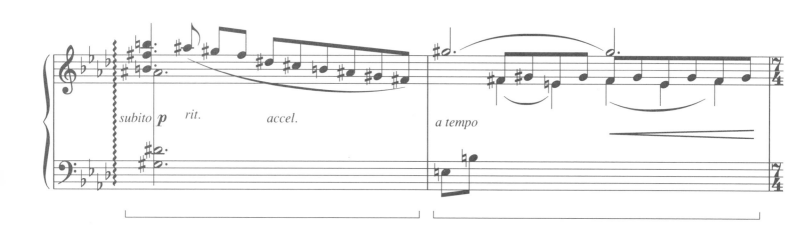

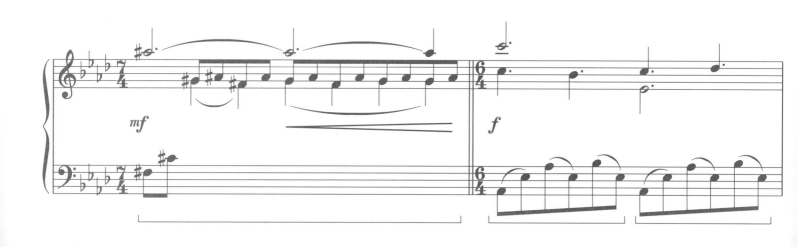

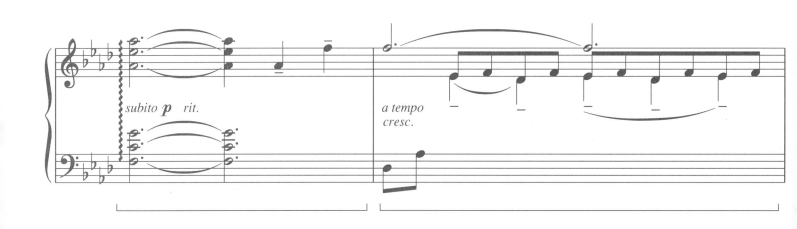

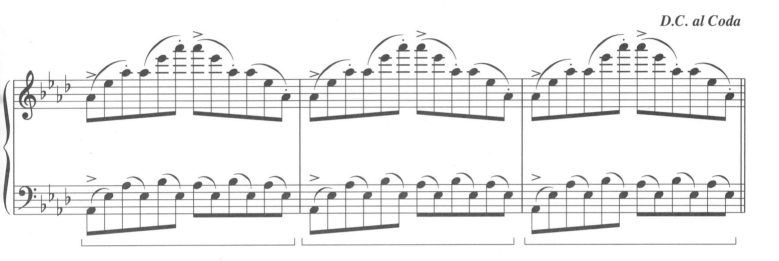

D.C. al Coda

Coda

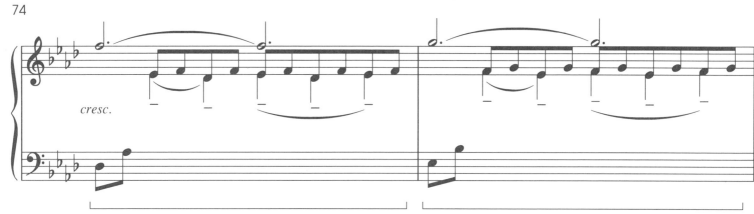

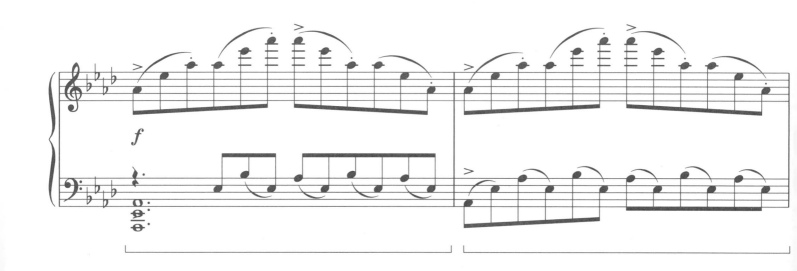

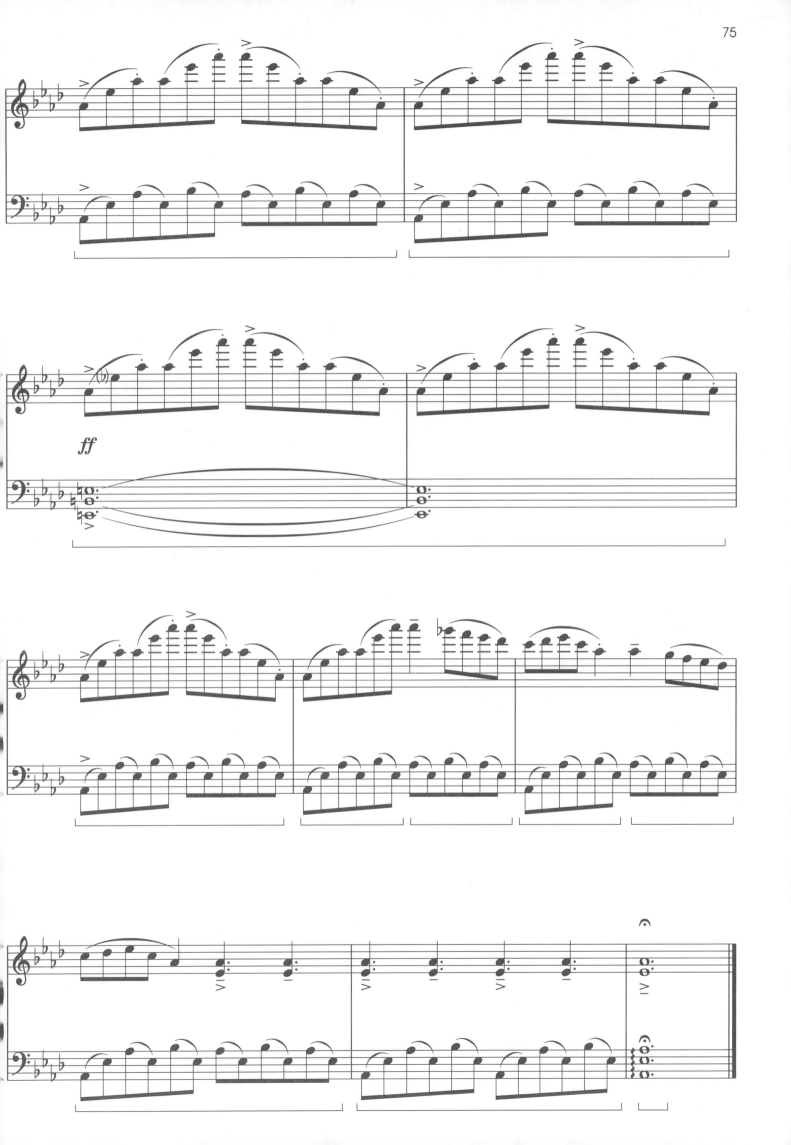

RAIN

Big Caribbean raindrops danced before my eyes while I wrote this piece

By SUZANNE CIANI

Quickly, flowing

♩. = 115 to 130

mf

sim.

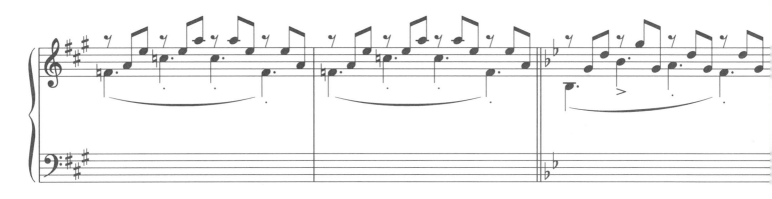

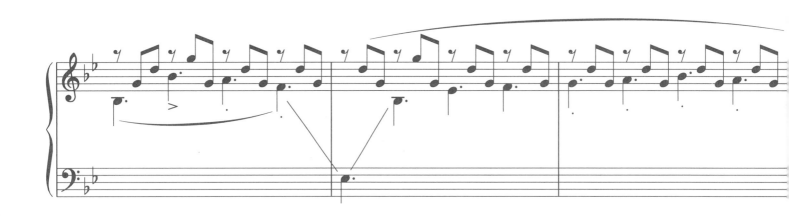

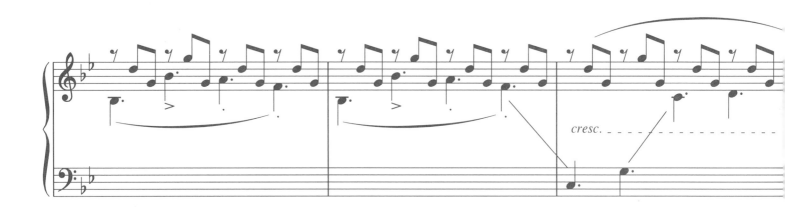

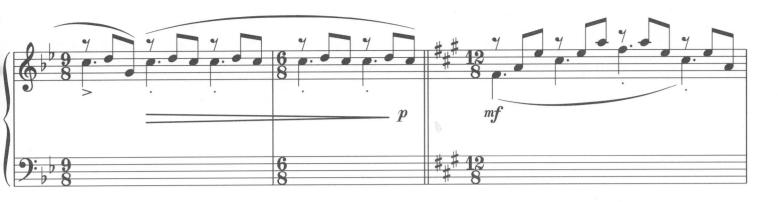

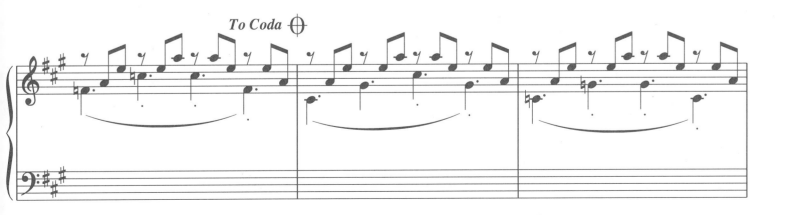

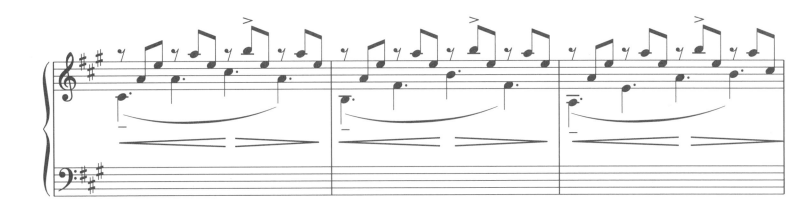

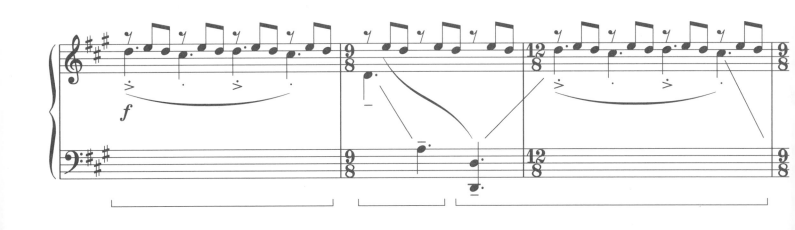

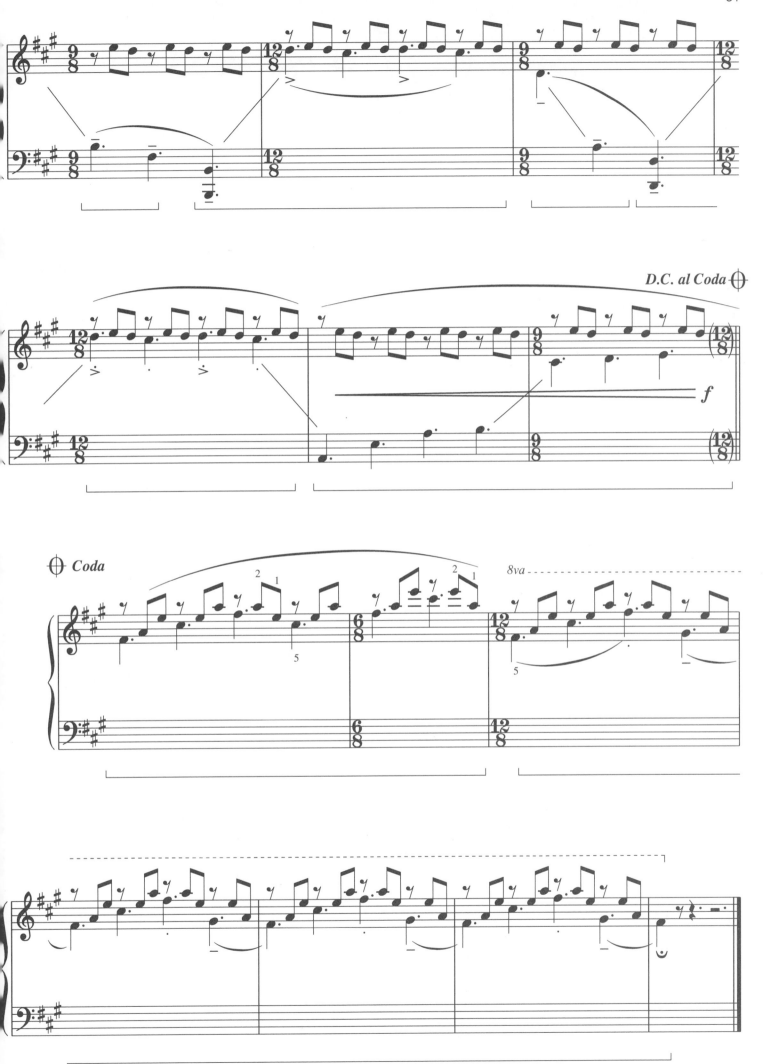

SUMMER'S DAY

Lazy times in the recurring poetry of summer...

By SUZANNE CIANI

sim.

To Coda 🔸

C

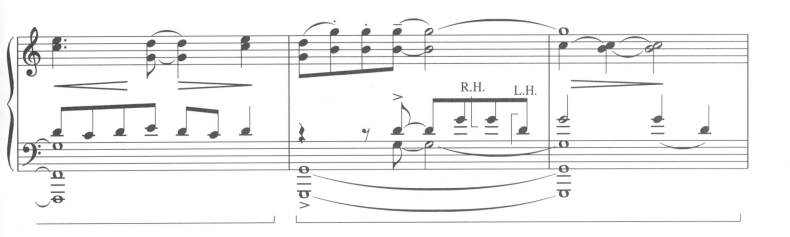

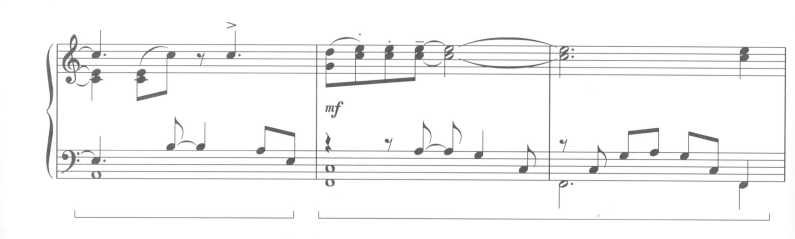

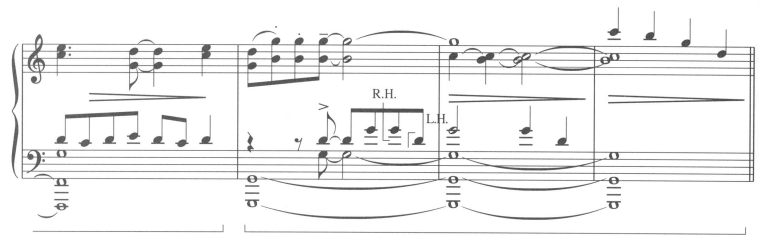

Coda

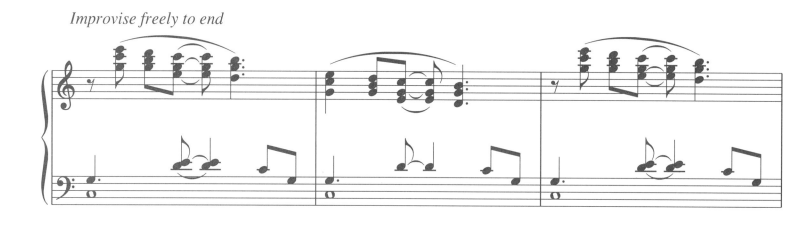

Improvise freely to end

TERRA MESA

The vast landscape of the Grand Canyon echoes through this composition. Time. Dimension.

By SUZANNE CIANI

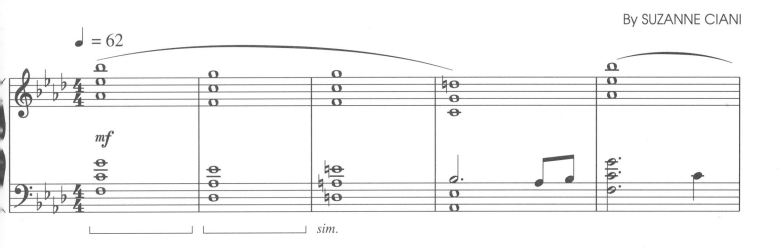

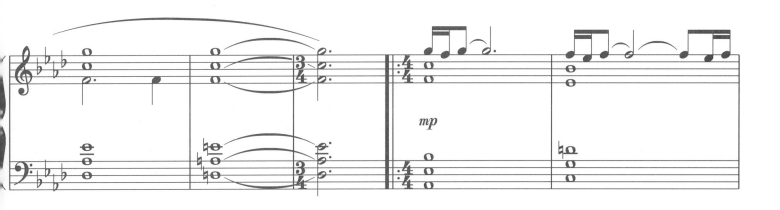

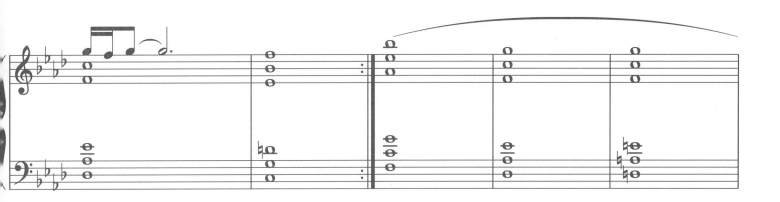

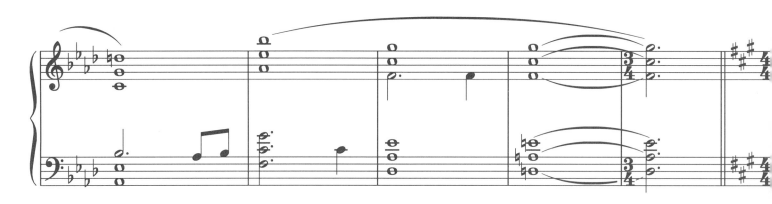

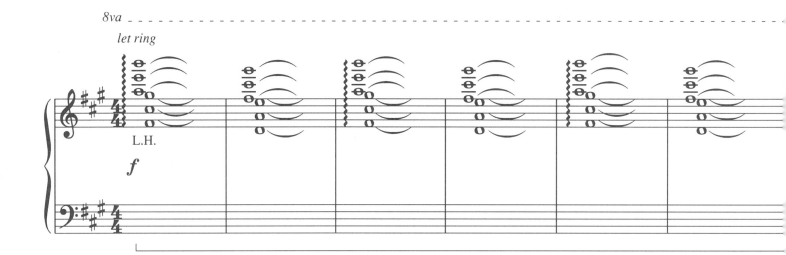

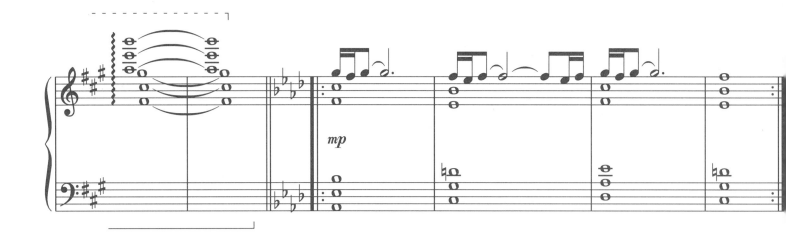

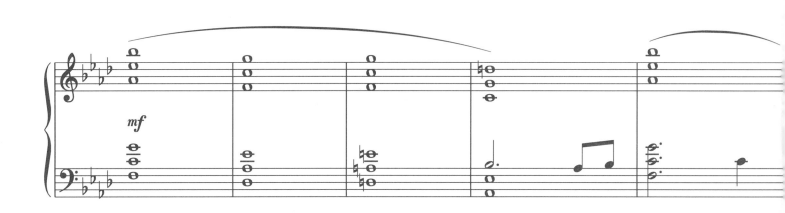

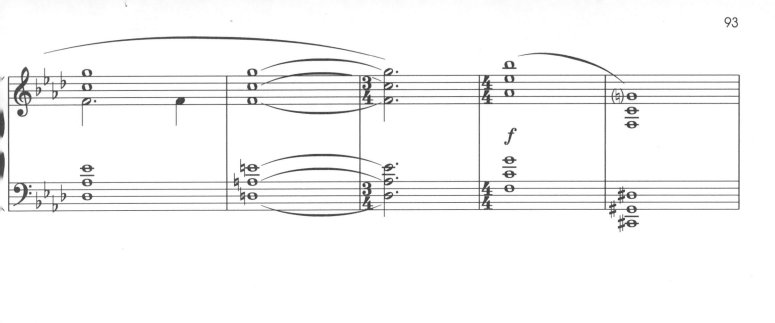

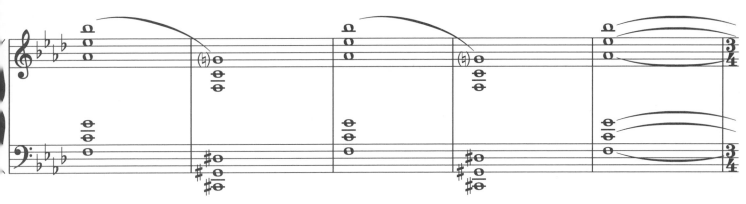

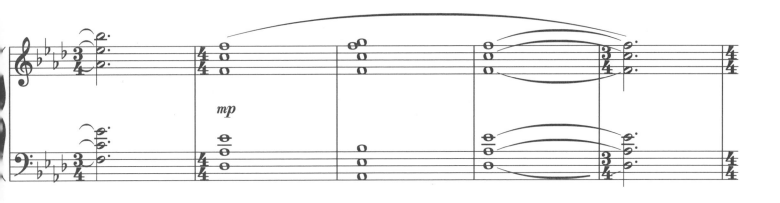

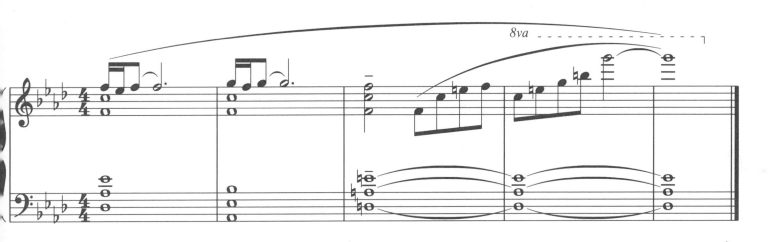

TUSCANY

Being Italian, Italy is a place I always seem to long for - especially the hills of Tuscany.

By SUZANNE CIAN

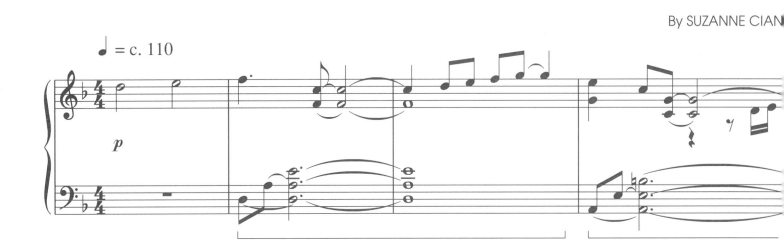

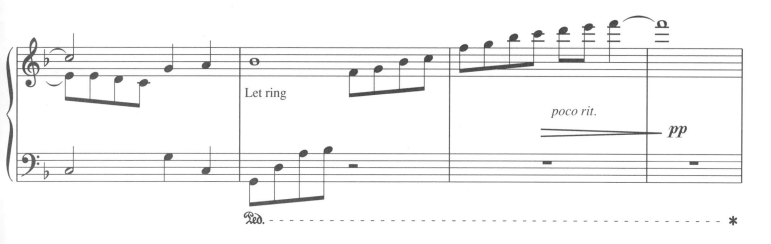

Let ring

poco rit.

pp

Ped. - *

mf
a tempo

p

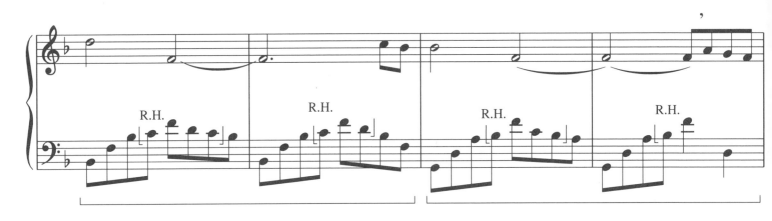

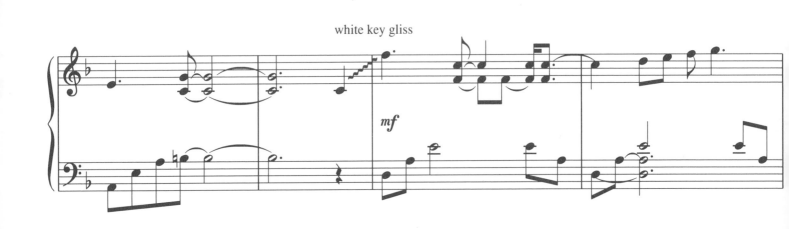

THE VELOCITY
OF LOVE

"Slowly, slowly, with the velocity of love..."

By SUZANNE CIANI

Moderately

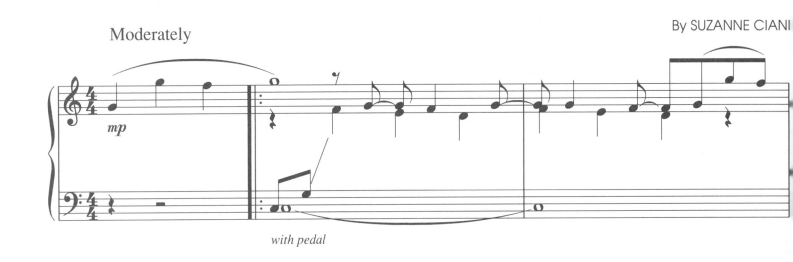

mp

with pedal

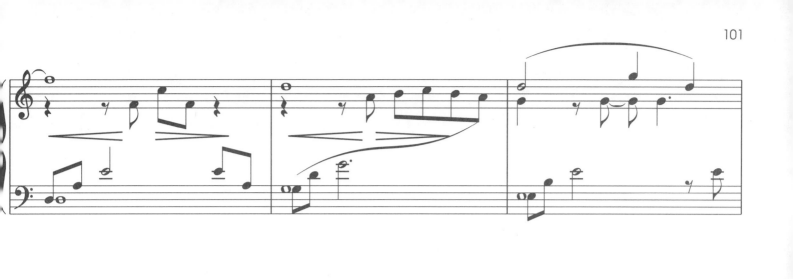

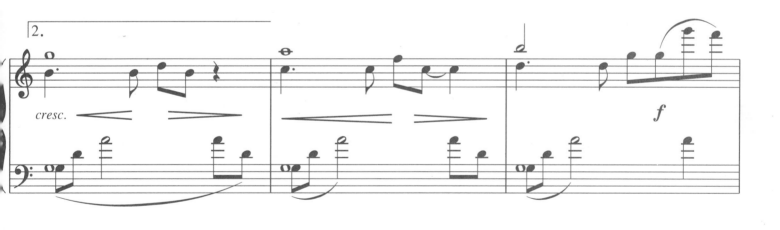

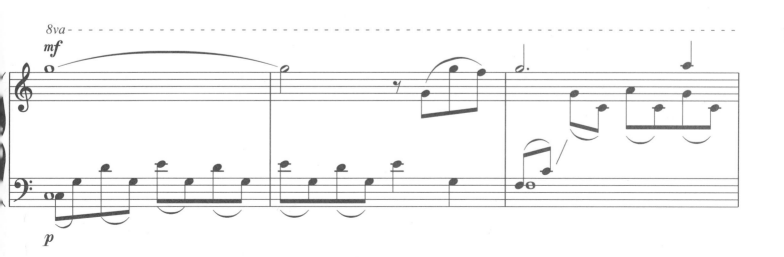

5

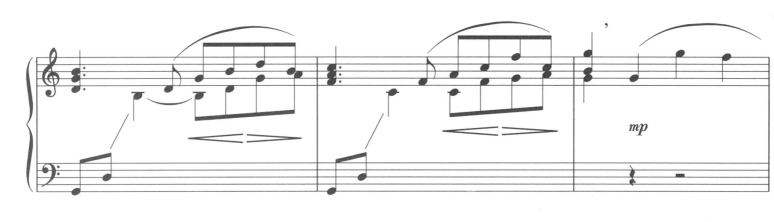

WHEN LOVE DIES

*A Greek Chorus opens and closes this story of the passing of
time and romance.*

By SUZANNE CIAN

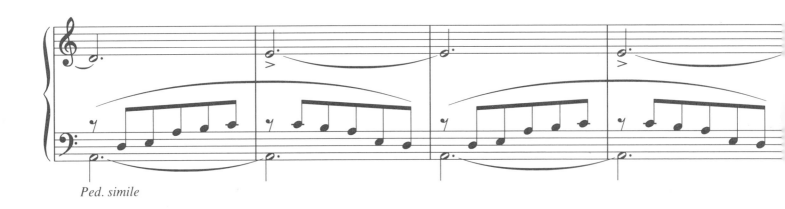

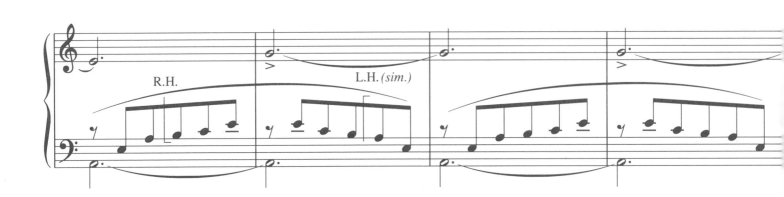

C

bring out melody

D

more lively

R.H.

cresc.- - - - - - - - - - - - - - - -

R.H.   L.H.

R.H.   L.H.

To Coda

E

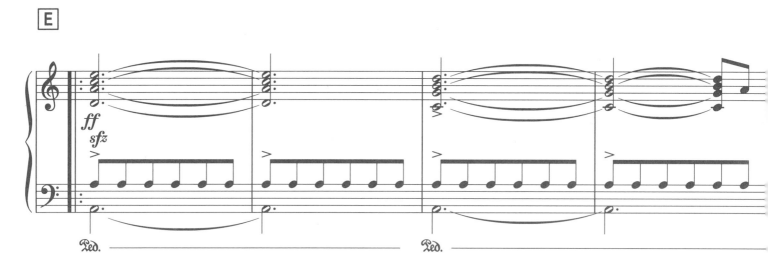

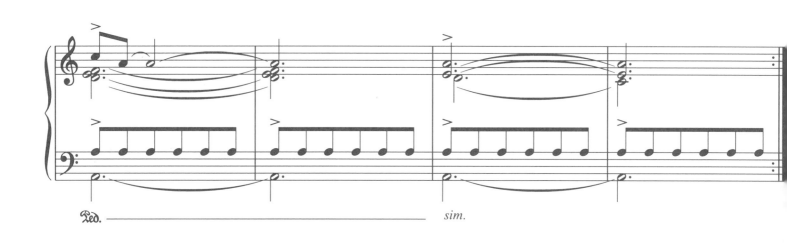

*(Be sure to stay in $\frac{3}{4}$ not $\frac{6}{8}$)

subito *p* R.H.

D.S. al Coda

R.H.   R.H.   R.H.